The song ended and the D.J. announced the next would be a slow one and that it was time to find a partner or cuddle up to the one you're with.

"Do you want it to be over?" Megan asked, praying the answer would be yes. Rafferty deserved someone better.

"With Emily?"

"Yes."

"Of course I do. I just can't believe she's here."

"Then dance with me," Megan said, holding out her arms.

"Megan, it's a slow song," Rafferty said, turning slightly red.

"So?" Megan knew she was pushing, but with Rafferty one had to be aggressive or she would slip through your fingers. She wanted to hold her. She wanted to feel her body close.

"And you're a straight woman in a gay bar."

"And you need to lose an old girlfriend," Megan said, grabbing Rafferty as the music began. Rafferty did not protest, Megan noted. This was a step in the right direction.

"This is not good." Rafferty glanced nervously over Megan's shoulder.

"I don't know about that. You smell really good and you have a nice butt." Megan slid her hand down Rafferty's backside.

"I think you're pushing boundaries."

"You can sue me in the morning," Megan said, pulling her closer and thinking this was the nicest slow dance she'd had in a while.

Visit

Bella Books

at

BellaBooks.com

or call our toll-free number

1-800-729-4992

Talk of the Town Too

BY
SAXON BENNETT

Bella
BOOKS

2004

Bella Books, Inc.
P.O. Box 10543
Tallahassee, FL 32302

Printed in the United States of America on acid-free paper
First Edition

Editor: Christi Cassidy
Cover designer: Bonnie Liss (Phoenix Graphics)

ISBN 1-931513-77-5

To my Beloved for her love and patience.
It's hard raising a proper lesbian.

Acknowledgments

I have to give thanks and praise for the undying support and patience of my editor, Christi Cassidy. Christi's eye for detail is impeccable and her ability to straighten out my fictional muddles is amazing. Despite the tumultuous nature of our relationship, she is always right. She keeps me focused, on task and exacts a sense of discipline from somewhere in my wily nature that amazes even me.

Chapter One

It was a hot April morning in Phoenix, Arizona. Gigi Montaigne sat on the front porch of her white stucco house. She put on her faded black high-top sneakers after she had given them a good shake to make sure there were no cockroaches lurking in their depths. One traumatic experience was enough, and now she always shook out her sneakers. She went to get her bike that was stashed behind the faded red Ford pickup that now served as an ornament in the driveway. The last time she had the truck towed home she vowed never again to stand by while the mechanic peered in at the engine and made weird noises that always cost her a lot of money. She had parked the truck and bought a very nice mountain bike, which was promptly stolen. From then on she purchased crappy bikes from the thrift store and charted how many days it took before someone stole them. Now it was a game. This bike was a clunker from the Fifties and had lasted exactly thirty-one days in her possession. This was longer than most of her girlfriends, except for Alex, an ex-lover who'd lasted months into years.

Gigi looked wistfully over at the dead jojoba bush that lay uprooted in the front yard. Alex had run it over trying to get Mallory to the hospital after she had walked through the closed sliding glass door. This happened a year ago, when Mallory found out that Gigi had had a torrid affair with Mallory's girlfriend, Caroline, and was the reason behind Caroline's sudden disappearance five years ago and her reappearance nine months ago.

Gigi's whole house was a testimony to her guilt-ridden, tumultuous past. Now Caroline was staying at her house, and if her guilt could incarnate itself and sit in her living room each evening when she came home, that's what Caroline was to her.

As she rode off Gigi glanced at the house again. Her grandmother had left her the money to buy a house because she hated the nasty apartments Gigi had lived in after her mother threw her out of the house for being gay, for being an abomination against God. Her grandmother had died two years ago, and Gigi still missed her and thought about her often. Her mother, Rose, was a staunch Roman Catholic and her daughter had become everything she feared. They were no longer speaking. Gigi was not speaking to Alex, either, or to Mallory, or to Caroline—or rather, they weren't speaking to her. It was like she was walking through her world with ciphers for companions.

She rode down the sidewalk on Indian School, for to brave the car-laden street was to flirt with suicide. Gigi always stuck to the sidewalk. As she passed under an overgrown, pigeon-infested queen palm tree, a bird pooped on her shoulder. Her white T-shirt now looked like a piece of a Jackson Pollock painting with odd strands of brown, gray and yellow. Gigi stopped and looked up.

"You stupid motherfucker," she screamed up at the tree and the bird. "Neither one of you is indigenous to this place so what are you doing here in the first place?"

A passerby in a car leaned over and said, "Actually, the pigeons were brought over from Europe in hopes they would be a good food source for the poor people living in the newly developed cities after they had been forced off their farmland. I don't know about the palm trees, probably some botanist trying to give the place a sense of the grandeur that other Western towns lacked."

Gigi grunted at him and nearly got run over crossing the street. By the time she got to work at Danielle Morgan's Photography Studio she was fit to be tied.

"What the hell happened to you?" Danielle asked as Gigi leaned over the sink in the photo lab and tried to scrub the pigeon shit off her shoulder.

"I'm not having a good day," Gigi muttered.

"Is that bird poop?"

"Yes, as a matter of fact it is, from an immigrant pigeon from the era of the robber barons."

Danielle laughed. "I didn't realize we had pedigree pigeons here."

"Neither did I until some stupid fuck in a car gave a history lesson after the incident."

"Only here, in wacko land, would that happen. Have you seen the latest aura photos we took the other day?"

"No, I've been kind of busy trying to get poop off."

"Here let me help you—oh, no."

"What?" Gigi said, getting panicked.

"It's in your hair."

Gigi looked at her boss. Danielle had long, dark, curly hair that framed her Madonna-like face. At forty-five, she was in a long-term relationship with a woman she was madly in love with. She played soccer every week and had a great body. Gigi wanted to grow up to be just like her. "You know this growing-my-hair-out thing isn't working."

"It is. You just have to get it past your ears and then you can tuck it back. Look, you started with no hair, and that spiky look has really gone by the wayside. Trust me."

"You know, if you weren't my mentor I'd still be selling dildos at the Castle Boutique, cruising women and having spiky hair," Gigi replied.

"That's why you came in for counseling at the Women's Center and that's why you met me. You needed to change, Gigi."

"I know. Speaking of counseling, remember I have my appointment with Dr. Kohlrabi at three."

"I know. We just have to get through twenty-five pimply-faced seniors before then."

"I still think dildos are better."

Danielle smiled. "I never said change was easy or fun."

"Did I tell you I talked to God last night?"

"Now, that is a good thing."

Later that afternoon Gigi sat in Dr. Kolhrabi's office studying the African masks on the wall. She decided that they gave her the creeps. She understood the point of them being there. Freud had had them in his office. Dr. Kohlrabi's office was a direct descendant of Freud's with its heavy old desk, leather couch and wing-back chairs. It was a therapy thing but it did not inspire confidence. Freud, she decided, was a pervert with weird ideas about women. At least Helen Kohlrabi was easy on the eyes. She was in her late forties, had shoulder-length blonde hair and soft brown eyes, and she was thin. She wore these little red plastic glasses over which she looked at you. Still, Mallory appeared to have been cured, so Gigi felt obligated to give this a try. Her life was still in shambles and she needed it fixed. She missed Mallory, she didn't know what to do about Caroline, and in some strange way she missed fighting with her mother. To top this off, God had visited her.

"So what's been going on lately?" Dr. Kohlrabi asked, apparently noticing Gigi's agitation.

"The usual messed-up stuff that keeps me from living a full life," Gigi replied.

4

"And what would that be?" Dr. Kohlrabi inquired.

"I haven't said anything to anyone because it's too weird."

"Isn't that what I'm for?"

"Yes and no," Gigi said, squirming uncomfortably on the leather couch. She was always hot from riding her bike and her thighs stuck to the leather. It was 100 degrees outside, dry but hot. She pulled at her shorts.

"Why don't you just tell me what's bothering you and we can sort through this together," Dr. Kohlrabi gently prodded.

"You have to promise you won't laugh," Gigi replied.

"It would be very unprofessional of me to exhibit jocularity," Dr. Kohlrabi assured her.

"What?"

"I won't laugh," Dr. Kohlrabi said. She picked up her pen and a yellow legal pad.

"I talked to God last night."

"Lots of people speak to God, in prayer, in interior monologues, in delusions. What kind was yours?"

"Not like any of those. One minute I was asleep on the couch and the next minute I was standing out in the middle of nowhere, like some Martian landscape, talking to God."

"You were asleep and dreaming. Why do you find that so alarming?"

"I had my shoes on and they were covered in soil, the same kind of soil that I was standing on talking to God."

"Do you usually sleep with your shoes on?"

"No, but nowadays I sleep whenever I can fall asleep. I was on the couch and next thing you know I had dozed off, drooled on the arm of the couch and had a little chitchat with the big lady upstairs."

"God is a woman?" Dr. Kohlrabi asked, raising her eyebrows.

"According to God, she is whatever you want her to be. As she puts it, she becomes eye candy. For me she became a compilation of dykes fashionably dressed in Tommy Hilfiger."

"God is a lesbian," Dr. Kohlrabi said.

"Does that rock your Orthodox Jewish world a little to the left?" Gigi asked, actually curious.

"As I have told you I'm an agnostic Jew," Dr. Kohlrabi said, peering over the top of her glasses. "And we're not here to talk about me."

"Oh, that's right. Well, God says she doesn't really have a body, or gender, or sexual orientation, but she does feel closest to women because they're more intuitive. She doesn't quite get how all the priests are men when they're so void of the spirituality that comprises life." To her own ears it sounded as if she were describing some casual conversation she'd had with a friend.

"Did you ask God any particular questions?" Dr. Kohlrabi was still jotting down what Gigi had said.

"Yeah, I asked her why we're here. I figured I owed it to the philosophy majors. I used to date a woman who was always yammering on about the purpose of life."

"And what did she say?"

"She asked me if I remembered that beer campaign that used the line 'Why ask Why.' She came up with that and slipped the hint to an advertising guy. She thought it was pretty funny."

Dr. Kohlrabi looked up from her notes. "What do you think that means?"

"I think that everything is just here, like God is here, like the universe is here. God doesn't know why she exists any more than we do. We're all just part of it."

"Does that make you feel better?"

Gigi thought about it for a moment. "It does. Not that I was pondering the question much. You know I'm basically an eat, sleep, shit and fuck kind of girl."

"I see," Dr. Kohlrabi replied rather tersely.

Gigi glanced up at the clock. "Well, I got to go," she said.

"Your time's not up," Dr. Kohlrabi replied.

"I know but I'm spent," Gigi said, getting up.

"Got a date with God?"

"No, but I do have something to do."

"What might that be?"

Gigi didn't want to bring up this topic today, but she said, "I'm meeting my father. He wants to talk, but I have to meet him in undisclosed locations so my mother won't know. I'm off-limits, as you know."

"What do you suppose he wants to talk about?" Dr. Kohlrabi inquired.

"How I might go about patching up our relationship," Gigi said, reaching down to tie her errant shoelace.

"Is that possible?"

"Only if God makes me an Angel."

"Maybe you could ask her next time you see her." Dr. Kohlrabi set down her pen and pad.

"Yeah, like that's going to happen again. Do you think it was just a whacked-out dream?" Gigi asked seriously.

"That would be my best guess. But if it does happen again put a good word in for me."

"Sure thing, until next week," Gigi said, rubbing the belly of the Buddha statue on Dr. Kohlrabi's desk.

"Why do you do that?"

"For luck. A better question would be why does a Jew have a statue of Buddha?"

"One never knows what or who is truly a child of God."

"Covering all your bases?"

Dr. Kohlrabi nodded.

Gigi sat at the bar in the Hard Rock Café shoving a hamburger in her face while her father, Paulie, told her about her mother's latest attempts to reunite herself with the church. Gigi studied her father's reflection in the mirror behind the bar. He was a middle-aged man with a receding hairline and heavily etched crow's-feet around his eyes from spending so much time on the golf course. She was convinced he'd taken up golf just to get away from her mother. How they had sex together to produce her still boggled her mind. She couldn't even begin to imagine her mother in the throes of passion. She had her father's full lips and his eyes but she had her mother's nose. Thank God, for her father's nose was rather thick with a slight bulb on the end. Her mother's was thin and shaped like the Italian aristocrats of old.

"She's really trying hard to convince the church elders that it was all your fault."

"Great! So what do you want me to do about it?" Gigi asked, dumping a bunch of ketchup on her fries.

"She wants you to go to the bishop and tell him that you tricked her and then fall on your knees in penance," Paulie replied. He took a sip of his beer and then licked his lips where the foam had landed.

"That'll be a cold day in hell. Why couldn't our family have been Baptist or something instead of getting all caught up in this Catholic crap? If I was a Baptist I might be seen as a challenge, not as an abomination." Gigi tucked a piece of her hair behind her ear.

"I like your hair longer."

"It's really getting on my nerves."

"So the answer is no."

"That's correct," Gigi said, dunking another fry and popping it in her mouth.

"I think she misses you, you know."

"Yeah, right. I miss you, though. Maybe I could ride around with you on the golf cart."

"No can do. Your mother has spies at the club and they've been warned to keep a lookout for you." He golfed every Saturday and Wednesday afternoons at the club with his accounting partners. Her father was a number-cruncher and Gigi still couldn't balance her checkbook. Financial prowess was obviously not genetic.

"Damn it. She has her fingers in everything."

Her father smiled. "I guess we'll have to stick to clandestine meeting places."

"I love you, Dad."

"Take care, kid."

They got up and her father snagged the bill. They pulled on it until it ripped in half and her father got the end with the amount. "It's my treat."

"All right," Gigi said. She gave him a quick hug and left.

As she rode her bike home, Gigi thought about how she had duped her mother into bringing the church elders to an art exhibit she was putting on. It was supposed to be a show extolling the virtues of the Virgin Mary but instead it was a series of desecrations depicting how Mary had been used by the church to represent something she was not. Her mother had subsequently been shunned by her parish, her most valuable social circle. She had wanted to get back at her mother for loving her religion more than her daughter, but the aftermath was more than Gigi had anticipated. Even her father had given her a good talking-to but in the end he understood why she felt so much animosity toward the church. Her father had accepted her being gay without much ado. He had sighed heavily, coveted other people's grandchildren, and then went on with his life with a Zen-like stoicism that things just were the way they were. Gigi admired this about him.

When Gigi got home, she was relieved to discover that Caroline was teaching a night class at the college. Caroline taught classes in business administration to wannabe corporate executives. Gigi couldn't think of anything more boring. Caroline always wrote her schedule on the erasable board on the fridge, like Gigi cared. She was going to have to do something about Caroline one of these days but right now she was sleepy from the beers she'd had with her father so she lay down on the couch and promptly fell asleep.

"My therapist says you're a figment of my imagination," Gigi said as she sat by God on a big black rock next to a crystal blue sea. She wondered where they were—certainly not in Arizona. It looked like the postcards she had seen of Maine. She looked around for a lighthouse.

"Here we go again," God said, sighing heavily.

"I like this spot better than the last one. It's more restful."

God smiled appreciatively. "Maybe there is hope for you yet."

"Isn't that why I'm here?" Gigi said.

"Maybe," God replied, sticking her toes into the frothy ocean's edge.

"Why am I talking to you? Don't you have lots of god-fearing, religious zealots you should be out there creating miracles for?" Gigi inquired.

"You, being the diligent lesbian that you are, should know better. There is no fun or triumph in preaching to the choir."

"So you've taken a sudden interest in a lapsed Catholic lesbian who isn't entirely sure she believes in God?" Gigi said.

"Call me silly," God said, smiling.

"To what end, might I ask?"

"You are a lot less formal than Moses."

"Don't tell me you have that in mind." Gigi gulped, suddenly understanding the gravity of talking to God.

"No, that went badly," God said, studying her fingernails and seemingly remembering a bad moment.

"What then?"

"It's impertinent to demand things of God." God picked up a small pebble and threw it in the ocean.

"The Christians do it all the time," Gigi retorted.

"And it's very tedious." God picked up another pebble and threw it out into the sea.

"You're still most likely a figment of my imagination and you really need to work on your throwing arm. You throw like a girl. Here, let me show you." Gigi picked up a bigger rock and threw it hard. "You need to kind of throw it from the side."

"I never got to play softball with all the other girls." There was a twinkle in God's eye. She picked up a rock and mimicked Gigi.

"See, that was better," Gigi said as they both watched the rock plop into the surf. The tide was coming in and the surf was turning all frothy and white as it crept up the beach.

God wiped her sandy hands on the front of her khaki pants. Gigi just noticed that God was wearing a white cotton shirt with sailboats and blue marlins dancing across it.

"Nice outfit. Very fitting for the occasion."

"Thank you."

"So what are you going to do with me?" Gigi finally asked. The question had been burning in her mind the whole time.

"For me to know and you to find out." God sat back down and put her Birkenstocks on.

"You sound like a kid on the playground."

"Children are closest to God." God dug a piece of sand from beneath her fingernail.

"I always thought they tended to be little savages until we socialized them."

"Only the neglected ones."

"We should all do better," Gigi agreed, watching God's brow knit and her lips purse. She had nice lips.

"See, I'm rubbing off on you already. Oh, by the way, don't go near your mother for a few days."

"At present I'm not speaking to her, or rather, she won't speak to me. Why? Am I going to glow incandescent or something?"

"Let's just say spending time with God can produce curious reactions. Now go get some sleep. You have a few big days ahead."

"I do?"

God nodded coyly.

"To what end?"

"You'll see later."

~ળ~

11

In the morning, Gigi woke up rested and happy. Even if God was a figment of her imagination she felt good after they talked, as if the chemicals in her body were supercharged and she could do anything. She decided to try the one thing that might prove substantial. Every morning since Caroline had moved in nine months ago Gigi would get up and try to walk across the pool. The deal they had made was that Caroline would leave the house and her life permanently when Gigi had accomplished this. Gigi knew this was impossible yet she still felt obligated to try just to let Caroline know that she wasn't happy with their arrangement. When Gigi told Dr. Kohlrabi about this deal she had asked her if she thought it was remotely possible. Gigi reminded her of the shaman who could walk on coals. But so far all Gigi had done was contract an ear infection from plunging herself in the cold water each morning. This morning she stood on the edge of the pool and thought about God. With God all things were possible.

She had snuck outside so as not to wake Caroline. Sometimes she felt like a prisoner in her own house. She looked into the pool. It wasn't too dirty. She should take better care of it. When she bought the house she hadn't really wanted a pool, but it was almost impossible to buy a house in Arizona that didn't have one. And her house had actually been a model home when the tract homes in the area had first been built. That was thirty years ago and now her house would soon be added to the historical list of central corridor homes. So the property owners' newsletter had informed her. It would buck up the value of the house and raise her property taxes. The house had fallen on hard times in the last twenty years but she had fixed a lot of the disrepair, excepting for the pool, which badly needed to be resurfaced.

She took the first step and didn't sink. She took another step until she was standing in the middle of the pool. She laughed. "How the fuck does this work?" she asked the universe at large. She heard a mourning dove coo. She jumped up and down in the center of the pool and it was if she was standing on cement. She whooped out loud. Then it occurred to her that she had fulfilled the bargain. Suddenly, she didn't want Caroline to leave. It was if her heart went bump and everything she'd been denying came rushing to the forefront. Hurriedly, she walked to the edge of the pool. She doused herself with the hose and went inside.

Gigi found Caroline in her bedroom packing and crying. She was stuffing things in her suitcase without folding the clothes, which meant nothing fit properly. Gigi watched in frustration as Caroline dumped it out and started over.

"What are you doing?" Gigi asked, alarmed.

"I saw you out there. I don't know how you did it but I promised I would leave when you learned to walk on water."

"You must have imagined it. People can't do that."

"I know what I saw," Caroline said. She blew her nose.

"It was trick of the light. See, I'm wet," Gigi said, running her hand across her dripping torso.

"Don't lie."

"I don't want you to leave," Gigi said.

"Why not? A deal is a deal."

"It was a stupid deal."

"Then why did you make it?" Caroline asked. She sat on her suitcase and tried to get it to shut.

Gigi stared at Caroline's hopelessly overloaded suitcase. "They're not going to let you on the plane with that."

"I'll put the rest of it in a trash bag. It can be my carry-on. You never answered my question."

Gigi sighed. The moment of truth had arrived much sooner than she had expected. She never should have tried that walk-on-water stunt. "Because I thought it wasn't attainable and you'd stay until you got sick of me."

"Do you want me to stay?" Caroline asked. Her eyes narrowed and Gigi felt her piercing glare. Gigi squirmed a little.

13

"Yes." Gigi studied her ex-lover's tear-stained face. Caroline had deep brown skin, long dark hair that she wore in a braid that fell almost to her waist. Her light green eyes were large and she had a tiny nose with prominent cheekbones. Half South American and half Irish, she wasn't exactly pretty but rather striking.

"Why?"

"Because I love you. I'm not ready to be lovers yet . . . I still have to sort some things out. We could make some new deal, like learning to change into a cat or walking across hot coals, or turning a stick into a snake," Gigi replied.

"You're crazy."

"Thank you. Will you stay?"

"If you'd like."

Gigi nodded and then left the room.

Gigi listened to the front door close and then came out into the living room. The last ten minutes of her life had been extremely odd. She did love Caroline. She missed Mallory and she wished she could talk her mother into some form of acceptance. These all appeared as insurmountable obstacles. She decided on a task she had been pondering before these strange changes had begun occurring in her life. She hopped on her bicycle and rode to the hospital where Mallory's girlfriend, Del, worked. Del was a doctor Mallory had fallen madly in love with a year ago. They made the perfect couple and with Del's help Mallory had let go of her obsession with Caroline. Everything would have worked out fine if Caroline hadn't returned and spilled the beans. Gigi cursed that day.

As she pulled into the hospital grounds she kept noticing that a flock of white butterflies had been following her. There had been an infestation of moths and butterflies this spring because Phoenix had experienced a lot of rain during the winter. Still, people had stared as she rode down the street followed by butterflies. When she glanced back, it looked like she was wearing a long white cape. They flitted off as soon as she reached the entrance of the emergency room.

Earlier that week Gigi had run into Del's nurse friend, Kim, who told her that Del had left private practice and was back in the emergency room at the hospital. Kim had at least been cordial. Perhaps the lesbian community had forgiven or at least forgotten her latest transgression. Gigi kept thinking that if she hadn't slept with Caroline all those years ago, Mallory would not have fallen in love with Del and lived happily ever after, and from what Kim had told her that was exactly what had happened. Surely that was worth something. She didn't know exactly why she felt compelled to go and see Del at the hospital. Since meeting God, Gigi had given up on figuring out the inexplicable.

She walked into the emergency room and went roaming the hallways. She half expected someone to call out and stop her, but no one appeared the least bit interested. It must be slow here at carnage central, Gigi thought. She turned the corner to find a room filled with people, one of whom was Del watching as an E.M.T. slammed a man with the shockers. His body kept jumping but his heart had apparently stopped beating. A woman, probably his wife, and the doctors kept watching the flat line. Del looked at the woman and sadly shook her head. The woman started to sob. For some odd reason Gigi felt her own heart ache and a piercing sense of grief at witnessing the wife's sorrow. Then she heard the voice of God in her head.

"Go touch him with your forefinger, gently," God instructed.

What are you doing in my head?

"Listen to me. This is important. Go touch him. Now!"

Dead people give me the creeps. Gigi thought of her grandmother in her coffin and all the bad dreams she had had after the funeral.

"He's not dead yet." God's voice was steely.

But . . .

"Do it."

Del was standing in her lab coat, her green eyes filled with compassion, her brow furrowed. Her brown curly hair was wet around the temples from her efforts. She was trying to comfort the wife, and the others in the room were cleaning up the equipment, so no one noticed her go over to the man. Gigi touched his arm with her forefinger.

For one second Gigi felt her whole body quiver with a kind of energy she had never felt. Del and the wife looked over at her. Suddenly her arm was glowing with a faint yellow light and the heart monitor registered a beat. Gigi stood back. Del and the nurses slipped into action.

"We've got a pulse. Let's get him to ICU," Del yelled.

The woman had stopped crying and was hugging her, telling her thank you over and over again. "I knew there were angels," she said.

"I'm not an angel," Gigi insisted.

The woman smiled and kissed Gigi's hand.

Del stood staring in disbelief.

God whispered in Gigi's head, "I suggest you blow this Popsicle stand before anyone figures out what happened here."

Why? You don't want me to get crucified?

"Something like that."

Why did you want to save his life?

"I still need him."

Why did I only touch him with my finger? Why not put my whole hand on his heart?

"I can't have him sitting up and being completely cured. That would really look odd. This is odd enough."

Why didn't you just come down here and do it yourself?

"It looks better when a known heathen does it. Now, I don't really have time to explain the physics of divinity. You need to get out of here before someone gets wise."

"Gigi, what are you doing here?" Del asked.

"I—I came to see you," Gigi stuttered.

"What did you do?" Del looked at Gigi, her eyes narrowing.

Just then another doctor joined them. He said to Del, "Mr. Eichenbacher is doing remarkably well. It's always strange when they come back like that. In med school we used to call that the finger of God."

Del stared back at Gigi.

"I didn't do anything. I've go to go," Gigi said, suddenly getting God's drift that it was no longer safe to remain here.

"Gigi, wait! What did you want with me?"

"Please tell Mallory I'm sorry for hurting her," Gigi said, running out of the room.

Chapter Two

Dr. Helen Kohlrabi set the phone down gently in its cradle. Her daughter, Megan, had just broken the dinner date they'd set for that evening. Megan and her fiancé were to meet her at the Supper Club to discuss wedding plans. Megan told her that something had come up and they'd have to reschedule. What Megan didn't know was that her fiancé, Jeff, had called earlier, concerned that Megan had asked for a postponement of the wedding and some time off from their relationship. Helen tried to ease his doubts by telling him lots of people got cold feet, and perhaps Megan was simply dragging her feet in terms of truly growing up. Jeff wryly commented that at twenty-eight, with five years of engagement behind them, Megan should really be ready to be a grownup. He had been correct of course.

Helen picked up the phone and called her daughter again. The receptionist transferred her call. It was hard not to feel proud of her daughter. It was every Jewish mother's dream to have an overachieving professional in the family, but despite her pride she was still concerned. Megan was a workaholic and emotionally detached. These were not good things.

"Hi, Mom, what's up?" Megan said cheerfully.

"Megan, what's going on with Jeff?"

"Nothing."

"Are you breaking up with him?"

"No, I'm taking a break to figure some things out. Marriage is serious and I don't like failure. It's my life, and how I decide to deal with it is my thing. It's all under control. I'm due in court."

"Megan . . ."

"I have to go."

Helen sighed. She wondered if the divorce had made Megan a committed loner who was afraid of the intimate bonding that marriage required. There was plenty of statistical data that supported that notion. Megan had become a different child after she and Lars had split up. Megan had been witness to the affair Lars was having and after the divorce refused to see her father. He began his new family and seemingly forgot about her. Megan pretended to do the same thing. Helen knew she hadn't, but the two of them went on to create a relatively calm and comfortable home life for themselves. Sometimes it was a relief not to have a man around. She hadn't dated and it seemed Megan had kept hers to a minimum until Jeff had come around. Helen couldn't help but worry.

Megan Kohlrabi stood looking out the window of her office and watching the heat rise up off the pavement below. She never ceased to be amazed at how hot the summer could be in Phoenix. Sometimes she longed for someplace cool and green like Vermont, but having just made partner in Aragon, McPherson and Daughters law firm she didn't think she would move out of state anytime soon. Instead, she would go home and lie by the pool for a while, sip a cold beer and forget about the heat.

Rafferty Aragon knocked quietly on her open door. Megan turned around and smiled. She liked Rafferty, and they were often partnered on cases together. Rafferty was the boss's daughter but didn't act like it. She and her mother kept, or rather tried to keep, a professional air about them at work. Rafferty was lanky with curly shoulder-length red hair and looked nothing like her Hispanic mother. She had light hazel eyes and a pretty face. Where her mother was beautiful, Rafferty was more boyish looking. Currently they were working an immigration case for an American woman and her Brazilian lover. If they pulled this one off they'd go down in gay history as moving the mountain that allowed straight society to disallow gay relationships. It was going to be an arduous case, but the Lesbian Alliance for the Ethical Treatment of Women was sponsoring the lawsuit and they had a lot of subversive political clout.

"I thought you'd be gone by now. I was just going to drop off the briefs the Alliance sent over," Rafferty said, handing Megan the pile of paperwork.

"Great." Megan set them on her desk and opened the top folder.

"Don't you have a dinner date with the best man on the planet and your mother to discuss the big day?" Rafferty inquired.

"I canceled it."

"You canceled the big Friday night dinner?" Rafferty asked.

"Dinner, Jeff and the wedding," Megan replied, not meeting Rafferty's eyes.

"I see. Are you getting cold feet, or did you discover something bad about him?" Rafferty asked.

"What do you mean, something bad about him?" Megan closed the folder and completely focused on Rafferty.

"What I mean is that I was hoping the best man on the planet was not some kind of porno-freak or evil to his mother or something like that."

"Rafferty, you've got to stop listening to Dr. Laura

Schlessinger. It doesn't give you a very positive outlook on hetero-sexual life." Megan had caught Rafferty in her office on more than one occasion doing her work and listening to Dr. Laura on the radio. Megan was fairly certain this was a daily ritual.

"It's all I know. I've never been straight. But boy, you straight people do have it tough. You should hear the people who call in." Rafferty sat on the couch and took her shoe off. "I've got this horrid blister and it's killing me. Don't tell anyone about my fasci-nation with Dr. Laura. The pink Mafia will get me."

Megan laughed and sat down next to her. "I won't tell anyone and no, I didn't discover anything bad about him. He's still a won-derful man. I think I'm discovering some things about myself," she replied, thinking that perhaps she'd never been in love with Jeff and now as the big day drew closer she didn't have the guts to tell everyone that she wasn't sure about spending the rest of her life with a man everyone told her was wonderful.

"I see."

"Why do you keep saying that?"

"Saying what?" Rafferty asked. She had removed her sock and was acutely studying her blister. Megan knew she was doing this so she could appear distracted and avoid further questioning. Megan had seen Rafferty use this tactic with her mother, Bel Aragon, when the occasion warranted it.

"'I see.' Do you really, or is it some new linguistic nuance I have not yet discovered about you?"

"Perhaps we should go to dinner and talk," Rafferty suggested.

"I'll make you dinner at my place," Megan said.

"All right. I'll bring the wine."

"You never answered my question."

"I do see. I've been in that place. It's not a place I recommend. Jeff is a good guy. You should marry him and live happily ever after."

"*That* is easier said than done," Megan said.

"I think you should try."

21

"I want to but there's something else . . . I don't know."

"We'll talk later," Rafferty said softly. She pointed to the hallway.

Megan heard footsteps down the hall and she knew that prying ears were approaching. Eileen was the law firm's receptionist and Rafferty was convinced she also did reconnaissance for her mother. She was not to be trusted. They had both memorized the sound of clicking high heels on the wood floor. Eileen wore them every day. She was a trashy blonde disguised in a neatly tailored suit with a short skirt that Bel admonished her for daily, to no avail. Hear the clicks and nine times out of ten they were attached to that snitch's feet. Megan nodded.

Rafferty left and Megan turned off her cell phone so she wouldn't have to talk to Jeff, who she knew would be calling. She straightened up her office, made a few notes on her P.D.A. for Monday and then shut the door. She wanted to get to the meat market before they closed at six. Then she wanted to swim a few laps, take a shower and get dinner started. She was hoping Rafferty would be done taking depositions by six and could come by shortly after.

Megan stopped by the boardroom where Rafferty was and held up seven fingers to indicate the time. Rafferty nodded.

Later that evening, Megan was grilling the steaks and doing a poor job of it. Smoke was clouding up her eyes and she could not seem to control the spurts of fire flaring up against the searing meat.

Rafferty came over to rescue her. She opened vents, reorganized the charcoal, flipped the steaks and closed the lid. "They'll be fine," she said.

"I make great salad," Megan offered, thinking she was glad she had stopped at the farmer's market on the way home.

"Come sit down," Rafferty said, pouring Megan a glass of wine.

Megan took a sip. It was a full-bodied burgundy and she suspected Rafferty had raided Bel's wine cellar. Bel had impeccable taste in wine. "Is this contraband wine?"

"How'd you know?"

"We can't afford it."

Rafferty laughed. "She won't miss it for months."

"I don't have cold feet," Megan said matter-of-factly.

Rafferty smiled. "You know, that's one of the things I like about you. You never beat around the bush. You just speak what's true without any gloss, or tactful embellishment."

"It makes a lot of people nervous."

"Yeah, but to me you're a breath of freshness in a stuffy world of protocol."

"Thank you. Jeff doesn't share your opinion," Megan said. She couldn't stop herself from thinking that she preferred Rafferty's company to Jeff's, and this thought worried her. It was the beginning of her doubting process.

"Have you reassessed your options and suddenly found this one distasteful?"

"I have doubts about certain parts of my relationship with Jeff," Megan replied.

"Such as?" Rafferty finished her glass of wine and refilled both their glasses.

"I need a point of reference. When did you know that you were in love?" Megan said, sitting down next to her after she had checked the steaks. They appeared to be doing fine now.

"I don't know for certain. One day Emily walked into the room and I just knew. I looked at her and my heart just—I don't know—like everything kind of melted inside, and then one day she left and everything sucked," Rafferty said wryly. "So maybe love is as overrated as sex."

"Rafferty, I was counting on you to be a shining icon of what life and love could be," Megan said.

"So you're saying he doesn't move you?"

"Correct."

"Megan, finding a good life partner is not all about passion. It is more about making sound decisions. Jeff is nice, dependable, loving, and doesn't have really fucked relatives. He's a good catch. Go with it. In time you'll find that passion is overrated, or it'll come later. One morning you'll wake up and want to fuck his brains out. Just give it time," Rafferty advised.

"I don't think time is the answer," Megan replied. "I don't think we have a lot of passion in our relationship."

"Sweetie, you've been dating for five years. I think you're past getting wet every time he walks in the room."

"I never got wet when he walked in the room. I think sex is greatly overrated." Megan thought about the last time they tried, and she just couldn't. She didn't know why.

"You're kidding, right?" Rafferty asked in earnest.

"No, I'm not kidding."

"Wow, maybe he isn't the right one."

"What about when you first fell in love? Did you get wet?" Megan said, taking a sip of wine and thinking the demise of her relationship was a great way to find out about Rafferty's love life. Rafferty smiled. "We're not talking about me."

"That is pure and utter cowardice," Megan replied, disappointed.

Rafferty got up and stuck the meat thermometer into the steaks. "Let's eat. I think they're ready. And you're right, I am a coward."

Dinner was fabulous. Megan made a chef's salad and they drank another bottle of Bel's wine. Rafferty helped Megan clean up and then begged off.

"I have to get up early," she explained.

"And do what?" Megan asked.

"Oh, just some stuff," Rafferty said, rummaging around for her car keys, which Megan miraculously provided.

"You and your mystery life. Do you have a secret lover?"

"No, no, nothing like that. Just some stuff I have to take care of."

Megan couldn't help thinking that Rafferty wanted to get out because they were both feeling kind of festive and one never knew where that might lead. She always did that whenever they threatened to get too close. Rafferty had firm boundaries that Megan had yet to figure out how to cross. She tried anyway. "Rafferty, can I have a hug?"

"Sure, I mean, if you want one."

"I want one."

Rafferty drew her close. Megan could feel their bodies touch and just for a second she knew Rafferty relaxed before she pulled away.

"So I'll see you Monday," Rafferty said.

"No, how about Sunday for brunch?"

"What about Jeff?"

"What about him?" Megan said, staring at Rafferty.

"Brunch would be nice."

"Great. Call me."

"I will."

The following Monday morning, Megan sat at her desk musing over the wonderful weekend she'd had with Rafferty. She had managed to avoid Jeff all weekend. They had gone for brunch on Sunday and then Rafferty had taken her to West World to see a horse show. It was nice to see Rafferty so excited about something. The law was obviously not her passion. Eileen, the receptionist, came in and broke her reverie.

"It's FedEx and it just came in," Eileen said, handing her the package.

Megan opened the package and then went directly to Rafferty's office. They had found a judge who was willing to hear their case. This could be a major break for them. She stopped short at her door. Rafferty was inside talking to her ex-girlfriend, Emily. Megan stepped aside so they didn't see her. Megan hadn't liked Emily because what she had seen of their relationship had not been good. All Emily appeared to do was play mind games with Rafferty.

"God damn it, Emily, you can't just walk in here and tell me you made a mistake."

"Rafferty, I miss you. People make mistakes or have a change of heart. Maybe it takes something like this to change us."

"You walked out. You said you couldn't love a lawyer. I work too much. You knew that going in and now suddenly it's all right with you. That doesn't fly with me." Rafferty's voice was steady and devoid of any emotion. It was like she was talking to a client.

"I want someone who is driven. That someone is you."

"No, it's not. You need to leave. I'm sorry I can't get over losing you and then have you walk back in and it's everything is back to normal. My heart doesn't work that way. You broke it and I'm done."

"Rafferty . . ."

"I mean it. I want you to leave," Rafferty said.

"Rafferty, please, can't we just talk?"

Megan contemplated leaving. She knew she shouldn't be eaves-dropping on their lover's quarrel. Still, she was concerned for Rafferty. And now, as Rafferty stood in the doorway, Megan no longer had a choice.

"I'll call security."

"I'm staying at the embassy. You can call me there."

Megan ducked into the empty boardroom so Emily wouldn't see her. She waited a minute and then knocked on the door, saying, "We got the case."

"How much did you hear?"

"Not much," Megan lied.

"She is totally fucked," Rafferty said, turning to the window.

"Are you okay?"

"No. I thought I'd never see her again," Rafferty said.

Megan took a step toward her. She instinctively took her hand. "If you need to talk . . ."

Rafferty started to cry.

Megan turned and took her in her arms, letting her cry.

"That fucking bitch. What I ever saw in her, I'll never know," Rafferty said.

Megan laughed and then gently wiped her cheek. For a moment they looked into each other's eyes. "She's pretty hot, long blonde hair, tight ass and nice breasts."

"And she's a complete manipulator. Besides, she was stingy in the bedroom department."

Megan laughed. "But she got you there."

"I don't want to talk about it. So we have the left and the leavers." Rafferty found a tissue on her desk and wiped her eyes.

"Don't remind me. Can I take you to dinner?"

"I don't know. I probably won't be good company," Rafferty said, slumping down in her chair.

"Please. We need to have to fun. I have fun when I'm with you," Megan said.

"Why do I feel like a distraction?" Rafferty asked.

"You're not a distraction. You're a focal point," Megan replied before she could stop herself.

"That's not good."

"Says you. I like it," Megan said, turning and leaving.

They went to dinner at a Thai restaurant downtown. Rafferty had a hamburger while Megan enjoyed a combo plate of things she didn't recognize on the menu. On the way home they drove by the women's bar. Outside of the bar was a line of women. It was Eighties Night.

"What's up with that?" Megan asked as they waited at the light.

"It's the women's bar. They play all that tainted Eighties music," Rafferty said.

Megan made a quick right turn, sending Rafferty lurching into the car door.

"Where are you going?" Rafferty asked.

"To the bar. Let's go dancing," Megan said, driving through the back alley.

"Megan, it's a women's bar, as in lesbian."

"Exactly. I can dance with you," Megan said, scouting for a parking space.

"This is not a good idea."

"Where's your sense of adventure?" Megan found a spot in the back forty. She hoped she could keep Rafferty's courage up long enough to get her to the front door.

"I lost it somewhere along the trail of broken hearts," Rafferty replied.

"Now that we're both single I think we should have a mission statement," Megan said, parking the car. She leaned over and opened the glove box. Inside, she located a roll of Tums.

"A mission statement?"

"Yes, I think it should be a dedication to spontaneous fun."

"You're supposed to be getting married, and I probably need to spend some time with a cognitive therapist."

"This is better. Two martinis and a lot of sweat on the dance floor," Megan said, popping two tablets in her mouth.

"I told you that Thai food is hard on the stomach," Rafferty replied, pointing to the package of Tums.

Megan hoped that's all it was. "I know, but I've never tried it. I'm sick of sticking to routine. Thanks for being a good sport."

"You're starting to scare me."

"Wait, the night is young," Megan said, pinching Rafferty's cheek.

"Ouch!"

"See, cognitive therapy. Misbehave and I pinch you."

"I don't think your mother would agree with your methods."

"Come on. It'll be fun."

"If you say so," Rafferty said, getting out of the car.

Megan walked into the bar like she had been there before, paid the cover charge and ordered them two martinis. She scoped the dance floor and as soon it filled up she dragged Rafferty out into the middle of it and made her dance to Eighties tunes. Megan watched as Rafferty let herself relax.

"Oh, shit!" Rafferty said, suddenly stopping in the middle of a song.

"What's wrong?" Megan asked, still moving to the music. Rafferty had completely stopped moving.

"Emily's here."

"Where?"

"Right behind you," Rafferty replied, pointing not very discreetly.

The song ended and the D.J. announced the next would be a slow one and that it was time to find a partner or cuddle up to the one you're with.

"Do you want it to be over?" Megan asked, praying the answer would be yes. Rafferty deserved someone better.

"With Emily?"

"Yes."

"Of course I do. I just can't believe she's here."

"Then dance with me," Megan said, holding out her arms.

"Megan, it's a slow song," Rafferty said, turning slightly red.

"So?" Megan knew she was pushing, but with Rafferty one had to be aggressive or she would slip through your fingers. She wanted to hold her. She wanted to feel her body close.

"And you're a straight woman in a gay bar."

"And you need to lose an old girlfriend," Megan said, grabbing Rafferty as the music began. Rafferty did not protest, Megan noted. This was a step in the right direction.

"This is not good." Rafferty glanced nervously over Megan's shoulder.

"I don't know about that. You smell really good and you have a nice butt." Megan slid her hand down Rafferty's backside.

"I think you're pushing boundaries."

"You can sue me in the morning," Megan said, pulling her closer and thinking this was the nicest slow dance she'd had in a while.

Later that night, Megan was sitting on the couch replaying the night's events when the doorbell rang. She wondered who it could be. It was nearly one a.m.

She looked out the peephole. It was Jeff. It was awfully late for him to be up. He was a C.P. A. and was usually up at the crack of dawn crunching numbers. She opened the door.

"Jeff, what's going on?" Megan said, suddenly acutely aware that she was standing in the doorway, wearing only her long white silk shirt.

"Better you tell me," he said gruffly.

"I don't know what you are talking about," Megan said, smelling liquor on his breath. He wasn't much of a drinker.

"I know where you were tonight."

"Are you following me?"

"So what, are you gay now? Is that why you're breaking it off?"

"Jeff, I don't know what you are talking about. I went out with a friend."

"Is that what you call each other?"

"Jeff, she's my business partner."

"Yeah, sure." He weaved a little and reached out for the door-jamb.

"I think you need to leave."

"I think maybe you just need a little of this to set yourself right," Jeff said, grabbing her wrist and pulling her to her knees.

"You're hurting me." Megan was shocked. Jeff had never done anything like this. He was the typical stodgy accountant who wanted a quickie on Sunday morning before he went golfing, and that was all.

"This is what you need," Jeff said, pulling her face to his crotch.

Megan started to cry. No one had ever done anything like this to her before.

"You need to think about the choices you're making," Jeff said, letting her go.

"Fuck you," Megan said.

"That's probably what you need," Jeff said, leaving.

Megan slammed the door.

The next day a dozen yellow roses and an apology card appeared on Megan's desk. The only purpose they served was to remind her of the nightmarish incident the night before. It was as if Jeff had suddenly been abducted by aliens and been reprogrammed. He never sent flowers and he was never violent. She was beginning to wonder if she knew him at all.

"Isn't that sweet?" Eileen said as she fluffed them up on Megan's desk.

"Very nice. Can you get me one of those Priority Mail boxes we always have hanging around here."

"Sure," Eileen said.

When she came back, Megan was feeding the roses one by one into her paper shredder.

"Can they do that?" Eileen said, indicating the shredder.

"It appears to be doing fine," Megan said, emptying the first of the tattered roses into the cardboard box.

Eileen left, shaking her head.

Just then Rafferty came in. "Is that any way to treat such beautiful flowers?" she asked.

Megan could tell by her attitude that Rafferty was clearly hoping to dispel the obvious tension in the room.

"It is when they're accompanied by a restraining order and a returned engagement ring," Megan replied, neatly taping the ring to the front of the restraining order. She had called a friend who worked in the D.A.'s office and they had sent one over with a courier service.

"Did he do that?" Rafferty asked, pointing to the purple bruise on Megan's wrist.

"Jeff has been stalking me, including last night, and he'd been drinking, which he doesn't usually do."

"So he knew you were at the bar. I'm so sorry."

"It's not your fault." Megan taped up the box. She could feel Rafferty watching her.

"Then what did he do?"

"He grabbed me and pushed my face in his crotch. He was hard, like he was getting off on it," Megan replied, not meeting Rafferty's gaze. She was still mortified by the whole event.

"What did you do?"

"Well, I wish I knew martial arts because I would have liked to kick his ass. Instead, I starting crying and he let me go," Megan said, starting to cry and wishing she wasn't. She felt so weak and helpless. These were foreign feelings to her.

"It's all right," Rafferty said, touching her shoulder.

"I'm sorry."

"Don't be. You know what? Let's go away this weekend. We'll go fishing. Do you know how to fish?"

Megan shook her head glumly. She sat down in her leather desk chair and studied her neat piles of papers. She had a lot of work to do but she didn't want to let Rafferty down, especially when she was taking the initiative. Under any other circumstances, Megan would've been thrilled.

"It's fun. Fly-fishing. I know this great lodge we can go to in Sedona. I'll make reservations. What do you say?"

"Okay. But I'll need an outfit," Megan replied. She could go shopping at lunch. She loved good clothes and now she had an excuse to shop for something outdoorsy. She was imagining something between Dr. Jane Goodall and Martha Stewart.

"We can shop at lunch," Rafferty said, picking up the phone and dialing. "They only have one cabin left and it has a king bed. It's the honeymoon suite," she said to Megan.

"So?" Megan replied, as she wrote out the address to Jeff's office, knowing he would open it there without thinking about it.

"It only has one bed," Rafferty said, clearly flustered.

"I won't seduce you. I promise. You gay people are completely weird sometimes."

"We'll take it," Rafferty said into the phone.

When Megan and Rafferty came back from lunch with a variety of Popular Sports bags, Rafferty's mother, Bel, was standing in the reception area talking to Eileen, the receptionist.

"My, we had a busy lunch hour," Bel said, pointing to the shopping bags.

"Megan needed some outdoor clothes. We're going fly-fishing this weekend," Rafferty said.

"I see," Bel said.

"Well, I better get back to work," Megan said.

"Here, let me help you," Rafferty said.

"Rafferty, when you're through there will you stop by my office, please," Bel said.

"Sure, I'll be right there."

"What do you think that's about?" Megan whispered as they brought the shopping bags to Megan's office.

"I don't know but I don't think it's good," Rafferty replied. "Sometimes, working for your mother isn't all it's cracked up to be." She dropped the bags and headed back to her office.

Ten minutes later, Eileen came into Megan's office with a stack of papers and the afternoon mail. Megan looked up from her desk. "Thank you."

"So Bel's not real excited about you and Rafferty going away this weekend."

"What do you mean?"

"I overheard them talking."

"Imagine that," Megan said snidely.

"Bel doesn't want Rafferty dating you because she has such a bad track record with women."

"We're not dating."

"That's what Rafferty said. Because you're straight."

"Don't you have some work to do?" Megan said, studiously avoiding Eileen's gaze. She didn't want to give her any ammunition. They might not be dating but Megan knew that she was developing some strong feelings for Rafferty, and she didn't want anyone to know, except Rafferty. This was going to be a tricky course, but there wasn't a thing in the universe that Megan had pursued that she didn't eventually get. Rafferty wasn't going to be the exception.

Chapter Three

It was Saturday morning in Sedona and Rafferty was holding a cup of coffee under Megan's nose.

Megan peered up at her. She still felt groggy. "Are you sure fish get up this early?" Megan said, taking the cup of coffee. She sat up and felt the early morning chill in the room. It felt good to feel cold in the desert. Sedona was north of Phoenix and the climate reflected that. Megan drew the covers up around her shoulders.

"Yes, they do. We can come back later and take a nap," Rafferty replied.

Megan sat up and rubbed her eyes. She watched as Rafferty wandered off in search of her coffee cup. Last night they drank wine, sat by the fire and laughed about the stupidities of love. She had never felt closer to Rafferty and later they talked in bed. Megan tried to imagine it was a slumber party, but by the end, she wanted to hold Rafferty and whisper all the things she was feeling.

Rafferty had kissed her cheek and fallen promptly asleep. Megan could not help thinking that she would make the perfect girlfriend, if only . . . She was starting to ponder the politics of sexual orientation. After all, she was straight, right? Wasn't she? Before she fell asleep she told herself that having a good friend was oftentimes better than a lover. You kept them longer. This sentiment didn't last long.

"I think fish are completely crazy," Megan said, getting up and putting on her hip waders. She went into the other room, where Rafferty had put the bagels they'd brought in the toaster oven. It smelled good.

"Megan, you can put them on when we get to the stream," Rafferty said, opening a container of cream cheese.

"Hell no, I'm up and now I'm dressed," Megan said.

"You're not right," Rafferty said, laughing.

"Like that's something new. Come on. I'm ready to catch some fish." Megan grabbed her rod.

"You'll need some pointers on the shoreline first." She handed Megan a bagel with cream cheese.

Megan peered down at her outfit. "How do I look?"

"You look good," Rafferty said.

"No, I don't. I look green." She jammed her hat on.

Rafferty laughed.

"Maybe when I get some fish guts on my vest and a little river spooge then I won't look like I walked right out of the store. Look at you. You look like you've been to the river."

"I have been to the river but I promise to teach you everything I know by this afternoon," Rafferty replied.

The spot Rafferty had chosen by the creek was sufficiently hidden from the road to afford the illusion that they were alone on the planet. Megan liked this. It felt nice to get away, far away from the city and people and talk and noise. She couldn't help thinking that fly-fishing was the most peaceful thing in the world. Rafferty was definitely widening her horizons. It felt good to get away from work and stand in a stream in the middle of nowhere and hear nothing but birds and crickets.

Rafferty held Megan's wrist as they stood on the bank of Oak Creek. The sun was just starting to peek through the canopy of the trees, hitting the forest floor like a patchwork quilt. Megan gave Rafferty her full attention as Rafferty demonstrated how to gently flick the fishing line out into the stream.

"Even, controlled follow-through is the key," she said.

Megan nodded.

"Now try it on your own." Rafferty let go of her wrist and stepped back.

"All right," Megan said, taking her first stab at launching.

Megan studied the distance between her pole and the stream filled with the mythical fish she was supposed to catch. She flicked the rod. "Ouch!"

The line had wrapped itself around her. Rafferty started to laugh. The line had encased both of them like a silkworm beginning to weave a cocoon. Not to mention the fly and hook, which had firmly ensconced itself in Megan's butt.

"Where did it go?" Megan asked, frantically looking about for the lure and then pulling at her waders that were suddenly pinching at her.

Rafferty had untangled herself from the line and was now sitting on the ground and laughing hysterically. "It's stuck in your butt."

"Very funny."

"No, I'm serious." She took her sunglasses off and wiped her eyes.

"What did I do wrong?"

"You need to watch the end of the pole," Rafferty said, pulling her set of pliers from the front pocket of her hip waders.

"The end of the pole?"

"Yes. Where it goes the line will follow."

"Well, I certainly didn't want it to go up my butt," Megan said, trying to turn around and see where the lure was located.

Rafferty laughed again.

"I don't think I've ever heard you laugh like this," Megan said. "I don't know if I like being the cause, but if it makes you happy, I guess it's not all bad."

"Thank you. I haven't had this much fun in ages. Come on, we've got to cut the line and get you out of this."

"Please. Is it really stuck in my butt?" Megan carefully fingered the rear of her pants.

"Yes."

"How are we going to get it out?"

"Very carefully."

Later that night, as they grilled the trout they had caught, they laughed about the hook incident again. Megan had successfully caught three trout, of which she was extremely proud. The thrill of casting out and then patiently waiting for the fish to find your lure the most promising was thoroughly exciting, but even better was the look on Rafferty's face. She was proud of her and Megan liked how that felt.

"I knew you could do it," Rafferty said as they cleared away the dishes.

"I had a great teacher."

"So are you ready to do it all again tomorrow?" Rafferty asked as she started the dishwater.

"Only if we go to bed early. The crack of dawn comes much earlier than one expects."

"We'll go to bed early. Let's have a hot tub, then have a piece of that berry pie you bought and then go to bed."

"Now that sounds like a plan." Megan stacked the rest of the dirty dishes on the counter. "Rafferty . . ."

"Yeah?"

"Thanks for making me come this weekend. I'm having a really good time."

"No problem. You make a great fishing partner."

Megan smiled. She thought, *I'd make you a great partner if you'd let me.* She knew the time was coming when they'd have to have that talk and she was going to be ready. She was going to have to be if she wanted to convince Rafferty that going out with a straight woman was a good idea.

The following Monday morning, Helen Kohlrabi checked her e-mail and saw a note from Megan. She hoped it was good news. As a therapist she told herself that her daughter was a grown woman with choices, but as a mother she couldn't help worrying about her. She sometimes thought that motherhood was the bane of good decision-making. She opened up the attachment to find a picture of Megan and Rafferty standing at the edge of a stream holding two large rainbow trout. The look on Megan's face was one of complete and utter joy. She looked at peace with the world and so did her friend.

As a child Megan had had that look often when her father was still around, the look of a child who was still fascinated with the world. That contented look had been gone for so long that Helen had forgotten about it until this moment. She printed the picture off on photographic paper. She would stop and buy a frame for it on the way to work. She wanted to remind herself that her daughter had been happy once and that she had been an instrumental part of that happiness.

Helen thought about the day when they had gone shopping for wedding dresses. Megan tried on flowing white dresses, looking more lovely in each one, but Megan wasn't happy. She was highly critical and at times combative and they had left the store without making a decision. Helen thought this should have been a happy time, but instead it had ended in Megan's threatening to go to a Justice of the Peace and have the whole thing done with. Helen pleaded with her. They went to lunch and Megan apologized, attributing the entire episode to bride-to-be jitters. Now she knew better. Megan wasn't ready to get married.

When Helen got to work she called Megan at the law firm. "I loved the photo. You look happy."

"I was. We grilled the fish that night, had a fire outside. It was so peaceful."

"I'm glad. Honey, have you spoken with Jeff?"

"No, and I don't plan to speak with him. Why?"

"The printer called the other day about the wedding invitations."

Megan laughed. "I'll call and cancel the order. Perhaps we could have him change the wording and invite people to the not-to-be wedding. They can still have cake and Champagne. I'm sorry, Mom, but it's better to have discovered that this wasn't going to work out than have it end in a nasty divorce."

"I know."

"I'm sorry I disappointed you," Megan said sadly.

"Sweetheart, you have never disappointed me. You're making a decision that affects the rest of your life. If you think it's the wrong one then I commend your courage in changing your mind. Most women would go through with it because they had told everyone that there was to be a wedding. If the time isn't right, or the man, or your heart, it's best left alone."

"Thanks, Mom," Megan said with a sigh Helen assumed was relief.

At the weekly staff meeting Megan and Rafferty had a laughing fit that Bel did not take lightly, considering they were discussing a nasty divorce case where the husband had attempted to kill his wife by lacing her dinner soup with Drano and then claiming it was an accident. It was only nine o'clock in the morning. Megan's butt was killing her and she kept fidgeting in her chair. She didn't know how she was going to make it through the day. Rafferty obviously noticed and one thing led to another. After Bel thoroughly chastised them the meeting continued. They both lasted until Bel was finished and then left the boardroom in tears and giggles. Bel gave them a dirty look and left them to their private joke.

"It still hurts?" Rafferty asked, once she had stopped gasping. She wiped her eyes.

"Yes, it hurts. I'm glad you're getting so much mileage out of my misfortune," Megan said, rubbing her butt. She didn't want to go to the doctor but something was definitely not right.

"Maybe you should let me look at it," Rafferty offered.

"It's fine."

"I was the one who dug the hook out of you in the first place. I can look at your butt, and besides, if it's giving you trouble then you probably have an infection."

"I've tried to keep it covered and put antibiotic cream on it, but nothing is working."

"Let's go to the bathroom," Rafferty said. Megan noticed she looked around furtively.

"I can't believe I'm doing this," Megan said, pulling her pants down around her ankles once they were in the bathroom.

"Your shirt is kind of long. Can I lift it up?" Rafferty asked, standing behind her.

"Please, don't be weird. I like when we're together and we can't be that way if you get all freaky every time we get close," Megan said, taking a huge risk. She took Rafferty's hand and ran it up her torso, pulling her in tight. She felt Rafferty nuzzle her neck.

"Megan . . ."

"Just stay like that for minute," Megan said. She could feel Rafferty's breast against her back and it made her tingle.

"We shouldn't be doing this," Rafferty said.

"You feel really good."

Just then the restroom door opened and Bel walked in. "I was looking for you two." She stopped in her tracks. "What are you doing?"

"Nothing," Rafferty said. Megan could tell Rafferty was flustered. She quickly backed away from her.

"It doesn't look like nothing," Bel said, peering down at Megan's ankles.

"She got a fish hook in her butt and now it's . . . it's not doing well." Rafferty's cheeks were bright red.

"How did she get a fish hook in her butt?"

"Fishing," Rafferty replied.

Bel started to laugh and then Rafferty laughed as well.

"Is it infected?" Bel asked, lifting up Megan's shirt with no compunction.

"I think so," Rafferty said. Megan noted how she covered her tracks. They hadn't gotten that far.

"I'll say. You need to go to the doctor," Bel said.

"I'm not going to the doctor," Megan said adamantly.

"Why not?" Bel inquired.

"Because I'm sick of people laughing at me."

"Oh, well, that might be an issue. I have an idea," Bel said, whipping out her cell phone from her jacket pocket. She dialed a number. "Harold, I have an employee who just had a fish hook removed under less than sanitary conditions and now it's all pus-filled and gross. She won't go to the doctor. Are you free for dinner? Good, you can come look at her butt and settle the whole thing. Great." She clicked off and said, "See, all fixed. I hope you girls didn't have plans. I thought we'd have trout."

"Who is Harold?" Megan asked.

"The guy who courts my mother but is really a fag who can't get past his own homophobia," Rafferty said snidely.

"Rafferty, that was unnecessary. Harold is a well-respected physician who has some identity issues."

"Whatever. When is dinner?"

"Six sharp." Bel headed to the door.

"We'll be there," Rafferty said.

Megan nodded and wondered if Rafferty was as wet as she was from their brief exchange. No one made her wet. She found this to be an interesting sensation.

"I'll meet you at the house," Megan said, pulling up her pants. "I'd better get back to work."

"Yeah, me too," Rafferty said.

Bel popped her head back in the door. "Rafferty, I'd like a word with you."

"Sure." Rafferty looked at Megan and rolled her eyes.

A short time later, Rafferty stood in Megan's office holding a red rubber doughnut. Megan looked up from the legal brief she was working on. "What the hell is that?"

"It's a doughnut. Sam found it in his janitor's storage closet. You sit on it and it's supposed to relieve the pressure on your butt. I don't know why we have one but I thought it might help."

"Rafferty, that's so sweet. Sam has the most amazing things in his storage closet. He doesn't clean worth a damn but he does have a lot of equipment."

"You can say that again. Here, try it."

Megan stuffed it under her butt. "Oh, my, that does feel better. So what did your mom want with you?"

"Oh, it was nothing."

"Rafferty . . ."

"She doesn't want me dating you because I have a bad track record."

"And what did you say?" Megan met Rafferty's gaze.

"I told her she didn't have anything to worry about because you're straight." Rafferty looked away.

"I see."

"Well, I better get back to work. I'll see you at the house."

"Sure."

Rafferty left and Megan leaned back in her chair. This was going to be more difficult than she thought.

Chapter Four

Gigi rolled over in bed. She sat up and wondered how she had gotten into bed when the last thing she remembered she had been napping on the living room floor after having beers with her father at the Hard Rock Café. She had to pee really bad so she crept to the bathroom. She didn't want to wake Caroline, who liked to sleep in on the weekends. All the classes she taught, except for the one night class, were scheduled for early morning, so she had to get up at the crack of dawn every weekday. Gigi looked up and saw Caroline standing in the hall staring at her as she sat on the toilet.

"What?" Gigi asked.

"Are you all right?" Caroline asked.

"I'm fine. In fact, I feel great, except that I woke up really having to pee. Why?" Gigi asked, wondering if something had happened to her to which she was unaware. Life was suddenly becoming quite different.

"You've been asleep for two days."

"I have? I slept the whole weekend? That kind of sucks. I must have been really tired. No wonder I'm starving. Let's go have breakfast at the Good Egg," Gigi said, getting off the toilet, washing her face and looking into her bright shiny eyes, pulling the lids down to check for something and deciding she was fit. She brushed her teeth and smiled at Caroline. "Don't look so worried."

"I was worried when I couldn't wake you up, so I called Mallory and she and Del came over and Del checked you out and I'm really sorry but I didn't know what to do," Caroline blurted.

"That was nice of them. Did Del give me a colostomy?"

"No, why?"

"I just figured that since I was out it would have been a handy time to have it done and on my part well deserved. I'm sorry I worried you. Do you have time for breakfast?" Gigi asked sweetly, taking Caroline's hand and gently kissing it.

"Did God recalibrate you while you were asleep?" Caroline asked.

Gigi laughed. "Perhaps. Did she come by?"

"Who?"

"God."

Caroline frowned. "No, was she supposed to?"

"Not necessarily."

"Gigi, have you gone off the deep end?"

"Only of the pool."

"Literally," Caroline replied.

"Do you want to go out for breakfast? We could sit out on the patio, catch some sun and talk like we used to do."

Caroline stood silent.

"What?" Gigi said, shuffling toward the coffeemaker. If she wasn't going to get breakfast at least some java would help.

"I don't know if I can."

"Do you have work?" Gigi asked, cogitating on the fact that she wasn't clear on what day it was exactly. "It's Monday then, right?"

"Yes, it's Monday."

"Why aren't you at work?" She glanced at the clock. It was only nine.

"We're having in-session today."

"Oh," Gigi replied, having no clue what that meant. "So we could go to breakfast then. I don't have to work until ten-thirty."

"I don't know if I can."

"Do you have plans?" Gigi poured herself coffee.

"No." Gigi watched as Caroline straightened the place mats on the kitchen table.

"What the fuck then?" Gigi replied, getting frustrated. She would never, even with divine intervention, understand women. They want you to want them and when you do they no longer want your attentions.

"We used to go there . . . when we were lovers."

"So is the place tainted now?"

"Kind of tainted." Caroline looked back at her.

"Are you going to elaborate or am I going to go hungry?"

"Why do you want to go there?" Caroline asked.

"Can't we just go? I want breakfast and I'd like to spend time with you."

"All right then."

"I'll never understand you," Gigi said, suddenly getting all the insight she'd ever need to know about her ex-lover.

They took Caroline's burgundy Jetta to the restaurant where Gigi ate voraciously and Caroline spent a lot of time staring at her. Caroline played with her food and the whole breakfast seemed rather tense. Gigi gave her a hug good-bye and then headed off to work, relieved to be out of the restaurant.

"Is it true?" Gigi asked her boss during a break that afternoon.

"That you will never truly understand each other?" Danielle asked.

"Yes."

"You won't necessarily understand each other but you will learn to tolerate each other in order to get through the difficult times and moments. It'll be trying and yet rewarding but you will never know each other's minds even remotely."

"This means life will be hell. Do I really want to go to this place?"

"Aren't you living with her?"

"That doesn't mean we're involved," Gigi replied indignantly.

"Let's go outside and talk over a cigarette," Danielle suggested.

"Can I bum one? I'm in the process of quitting," Gigi said, taking the cigarette and running it under her nose as if it were a fine cigar. It smelled heavenly.

"You're always in the process of quitting."

"I can't decide if I'm a smoker or not."

"If you smoke then it would warrant that you are a smoker."

"All right. I'm a closet smoker. Now can I have the lighter?" Gigi noticed the swarm of butterflies that had appeared out of nowhere. They landed on the window ledges and the park benches.

"What's up with you and these butterflies?"

"What do you mean?"

"They only come around when you're around."

"Is this like the smoking thing?"

"Yes."

"I don't know but I'm getting kind of used to them," Gigi said, sticking out her finger and letting one come to light upon it. "Aren't they beautiful?" she said, taking a hard look at the fragile white wings.

Danielle chuckled. "That is slightly out of character for you."

"You mean noticing the universe?"

"Yes," Danielle said, putting her cigarette out and then lighting another one.

"I suppose it is. Are you implying that I'm normally so self-centered that I can't see beyond my own pie hole?"

47

"You said it, not me," Danielle said, laughing. "That's was one of the things I like about you. You are brutally honest and totally self-effacing. It's a breath of fresh air."

"I'm glad you like it. So tell me what real love is supposed to be like." Gigi took a long drag off her cigarette. The beauty of periodic smoking was the giddy high it gave you. She was contemplating asking Danielle for another when she was handed another. She wondered sometimes if Danielle was not a mind reader.

"The thing to remember is that no matter how bad it gets, how much you rip each other apart, you'll always go back to the good place," Danielle sagely replied, seeming to relive some of those moments in her own life. "You know, with each passing decade of my life I'm learning to understand myself, and my philosophies are becoming more developed. It's a pity that we have to get old before we really get a good handle on living well."

"I seem to spend a lot of time in that ripped-apart place. What's the good place like?" Gigi asked, uncertain that she had ever known this particular place in any of her relationships.

"It's past lust and infatuation. You become friends, lovers and companions. You learn to understand each other, love each other beyond condition," Danielle said, folding her hands together to illustrate her point.

"Does that mean you still have sex?"

"You are so crass. As a matter of fact we do. We make love a lot, contrary to people's notions that long-term relationships always suffer lesbian bed death. I'm doing it more than you are at the moment."

"I resent that."

"The truth is often unkind."

"Do you think I should stick it out with Caroline? I am emotionally challenged." Gigi watched the cloud of white butterflies performing a synchronized flight pattern.

"How does she make you feel?"

"Part of me wants to jump her bones, part of me wants to be her best friend, and the rest thinks she should walk out because I don't deserve her."

"I think you stand a chance," Danielle said, snuffing out her cigarette and opening the shop door for Gigi.

The rest of the afternoon was slow and Gigi spent most of it building small metal sculptures out of paperclips. Danielle got disgusted and let her go for the rest of the afternoon.

Gigi headed over to the flower shop on Central Avenue. She had spent the afternoon pondering what Danielle had said about relationships. Gigi had never been in a flower shop in her life and she felt distinctly out of place. It reminded her of going to the God's Word shop with her mother to buy religious items after Gigi had spent the night before with her Aunt Lil wrecking religious shrines, her mother's included. It must be how Satan felt in a church . . . uncomfortable and out of place. While she was involved in her mental machinations she nearly plowed down a woman who was aimlessly wandering through the maze of flower pots.

"Mallory!" Gigi said before she could stop herself. She instantly panicked. The flower shop was warm and kind of sticky. She began to sweat.

"Gigi, what are you doing here?" Mallory asked, obviously as upset as Gigi was with this surprise meeting.

"Buying flowers."

"Oh, yes, of course," Mallory said.

Gigi watched as Mallory fingered the petals of a bunch of yellow roses.

"You have hair," Mallory said. "I have never known you with hair." She pointed to the mop that was currently riding on top of Gigi's head. Gigi knew it was totally out of control.

"This is true. When I first met you I had just completed my first home job with my dad's razor and you still talked to me." Gigi could feel her eyes getting a little misty at the thought of those memories of Mallory. She missed her horribly and no matter how hard she tried she couldn't erase the long years of their friendship.

"I did and it was a very bad job. You had little patches everywhere."

"I wanted a flattop and my mother wouldn't let me so I took matters into my own hands. She took me to the barber after that."

"Why the change?"

"Everything has changed, hasn't it?" Gigi replied.

"It has. What does your mother have to say about your growing out your hair?"

"She's still not speaking to me, you know, after the art show debacle."

"I see," Mallory said. Gigi watched as she leaned down and stuck her face in a batch of red roses. Mallory loved flowers. Gigi always thought they were sort of stupid.

"You're better off now."

"Yes, but that doesn't make up for the years of therapy and mental anguish."

Gigi said shyly, "I like Dr. Kohlrabi."

"You do?" Mallory replied.

"She's the only person on the planet, aside from you, but you weren't speaking to me either, who understands me."

"And calls you on your bullshit."

"Exactly," Gigi said, taking no offense.

"Had any more of those spells?" Mallory walked down the aisle and surveyed the selection. Gigi followed her.

"No, I'm fine."

"I miss you," Mallory blurted.

"You shouldn't," Gigi said, feeling instant shame. She had never deserved Mallory.

"Are you getting Caroline flowers?"

"Yes, but I don't know what kind," Gigi said, looking around.

"Calla lilies are her favorite," Mallory said, gesturing to a bucket of white tube-like lilies.

"What does Del like?" Gigi asked.

"Sunflowers."

"I wish we could hang out," Gigi said, selecting a half-dozen calla lilies and getting misty-eyed again.

"We can't. We're not in that same place anymore."

"You could forgive me and there could be a new place."

"Such as?"

"Racquetball on Thursday after my therapy appointment."

"You play racquetball now?"

"Now and then. I kind of like it, you know, smashing the ball against the wall and trying to outmaneuver your partner," Gigi replied, hoping God would not take offense if she expanded her field of play.

"I don't know if I'm ready for that," Mallory said.

"Try it once."

"I'll see."

"The club on Central at six-thirty," Gigi said.

Mallory smiled. "You never give up."

"You liked that about me once," Gigi said.

God was sitting on the park bench waiting for Gigi when she came out of the flower shop cradling a bunch of calla lilies in her arms.

"I hope you're not mad," Gigi said, suspecting that God had been privy to her conversation with Mallory. Not being much of a Biblical scholar and remembering very little from her Catholic school upbringing, she was uncertain how much God saw and heard.

"Mad about what?" God asked calmly, rubbing the petal of a calla lily between her forefinger and thumb. "You know, flowers are one of my finest creations and I never cease to be amazed at their beauty."

Gigi thought for a moment. On any given day God could be angry about a million different things, considering the current state of affairs—bombs, rapes, murders, corruption, graft, adultery, child abuse. The list was endless. Gigi decided she'd stick to her own trivial world. "About my playing racquetball with Mallory."

"You can play racquetball with other people. It doesn't violate one of the Ten Commandments. 'Thou shall not play racquetball with anyone other than God.' " She chuckled. "In fact, I'm glad you've patched things up with Mallory."

"I still love her," Gigi said.

"And most likely you always will. Some things in this farcical universe do remain constant."

"Like physical laws?"

"To a certain extent, but I was referring to emotions and their manifestations."

"Why did you create love?" Gigi asked, suddenly curious.

"I didn't. It's actually a human construct and a very interesting one. I came up with primal urge and that was to ensure procreation. I think I may have overdone that one, given the current population."

"I don't believe it," Gigi said, disgusted.

"Look, I may have hard-wired human beings but I had no idea what you were really capable of. Your emotions are something uniquely human. Love, from what I can figure, emanates from you and you've taught other creatures to love you in return."

"Such as animals."

"And myself," God replied.

"You didn't create us out of love," Gigi said, feeling her cheeks burn, her hand tightening into a fist around the flower stems.

"You're squishing them," God said, pointing to the lilies.

Gigi eased her grip. She wanted to get them home in one piece. "Why are we here then?"

God studied her fingernails. She looked up at Gigi. "I was lonely and frankly quite bored."

Gigi's jaw dropped. "You made us because you were bored! That's just fucking great. I can't believe this. All this shit that has come down in your name, and there's no grand design. How can you walk past a church and not feel like a farce?"

"I do my best to avoid them. You see, much has happened out of something that was initially good. I call it the Law of Unintended Consequences. There seems to be a current that runs through the universe that allows for various consequences. A right action occurs from a wrong choice, a good thing goes bad, or a bad thing creates good."

"But I thought you were responsible for that," Gigi said, calming down as this bit of knowledge permeated her brain. The idea was big and she was not certain she liked knowing it.

"I can't get involved anymore. Things don't turn out right most of the time. So I'm forced to watch the travesty and sit on my hands. It's not an easy thing to do," God replied, lowering her head and looking suddenly sad.

Gigi felt for her. "You're involved now."

"But on a very limited scale, and this time I think I may have worked out the kinks."

"You think if you downsize, your plan will go off better?" Gigi asked.

"I'm hoping so."

"It had better. I don't want to be part of another one of your botched attempts to save the human race. If I were you I'd let us alone."

"Call me an optimist."

"I think you're more like an overindulgent parent."

"You may be right."

Later that afternoon at the office, Carmen, Helen's receptionist, came to tell her that her new patient had arrived. Helen took out her pad and prepared herself to meet a new client. For as nervous as the clients were meeting the therapist for the first time so was the therapist, for it meant starting at the beginning. Beginnings were always difficult.

Carmen showed Ms. Goldie Jahweh into the doctor's office. A thirty-something woman dressed in blue jeans and a Tommy Hilfinger polo shirt greeted her. Helen stood and shook her hand, then the new client took a seat on the brown leather couch.

"So what seems to be the problem?" Helen inquired, her pen poised to take notes.

"I want to know why you don't think I exist." She crossed her legs and peered intently at her.

Helen frowned. "I'm afraid I don't know what you're talking about."

"Perhaps, I should properly introduce myself. I'm God."

Helen blinked rapidly and said, "Excuse me?"

"I'm God. And according to Gigi you think I'm a figment of her imagination. I find that objectionable."

"You don't look like God," Helen ventured. She could feel her heart beginning to pound and wondered if she had a delusional schizophrenic on her hands or the real thing. There was no such thing as the real thing. She reminded herself of this fact daily.

"What should God look like? In your own scripture you were made in my image. I would think that as diverse as the human race is, I could be just as diverse."

Helen sat silent. The woman had a point. Still, God did not walk into someone's office and demand to be recognized. Helen waited, curious how the session would unfold.

Finally God said, "All right, I see there might be a need for some showmanship here. Let me see." As Helen watched she morphed into an old man who looked something akin to Charlton Heston in *The Ten Commandments*. He wore a long gray beard and flowing red robe. He zapped the jar full of pens into a bunch of swirling snakes. Helen jumped back as they slithered across her desk. This was scary and she couldn't find a logical explanation for it. The next thing she knew an elderly Orthodox Jew with a black hat and long curls sat before her, patiently waiting for her response. The pens had resumed their original form.

"I think I prefer your original incarnation." She reached over and gingerly fingered her pen jar to assure herself that they had become inanimate objects again.

God granted her request and assumed her original form. "Now, do you think I'm a figment of Gigi's imagination?"

"No, now I'm wondering if you're a figment of my imagination."

"Don't make me do more stuff. It's so tedious." God pouted.

"Please don't. I meant no disrespect, but you know delusions are part of the parcel when it comes to patients."

"Gigi's not crazy. She's confused and morally bereft. She *is* high-spirited, and that will come in handy for the task at hand."

"Which is?"

"For me to know and you two to find out," God said with a twinkle in her eye.

"So what can I help you with?" Helen asked, hoping this was something she could handle. Her mind was still boggled at having God in her office seeking counsel.

"I'm concerned with your lack of faith, or more specifically, everyone's lack of faith. I think I might be having an identity crisis."

"Perhaps we're in need of guidance," Helen suggested.

"I'm not falling for that one again."

"What do you mean?"

"I gave guidance once and it turned into something horrific. I need something subtle this time, something more covert," God said, picking up the small statue of Buddha that was sitting on the desk. She rubbed its belly. "I kind of miss the days of icons. He looks so happy."

Helen refrained from mentioning that God's icon was currently a tortured being hanging on every altar worldwide. "So what were you thinking might be a more covert way to get us all back on track?"

"I was thinking more along the lines of a self-help book."

"Are you going to self-publish or just zap it into bookstores?"

God laughed. "No, I plan on using an intermediary."

"But a covert one."

"Exactly. I don't think the world is ready for a Second Coming. I just want to help."

"Anything is worth a try."

"Can I come back next week? I think I might benefit from some counseling."

"I hardly think I would have anything to offer," Dr. Kohlrabi replied, thinking she couldn't possibly live up to this task.

"Why not?"

"You're God, all things, all-knowing and all of that."

"You're not the agnostic Jew you pretend to be," God replied smugly. "You see, I need someone objective to talk to."

"And you think I might be that person."

"You are a licensed therapist."

"This is true."

"We might learn some things from each other. Besides you don't really have a choice."

"So what do you want to discuss?" Helen glanced at the pen jar.

"I won't do that again. You're really freaked out, aren't you?" God crossed her legs and folded her hands.

"Well, it's not every day that the Almighty walks into your office and seeks counsel."

"This is true. I just feel like people don't understand me anymore. I feel like I'm absent from the picture. I'm part of it all, and yet I feel so disconnected." God frowned.

"Maybe it's time we all got to know you again. It's been a while, you know."

"I know. But I get so anxious every time I show up. Stuff happens I didn't plan on."

"Perhaps that's where we should start. So your current crisis is one of disconnection and anxiety about becoming involved again. Correct?" Helen made a note.

"Yes."

"Let's start there."

"I can do that," God said, uncrossing her legs and standing up.

"I'll see you next week then."

"Great."

After God left Helen went out to see Carmen. "How did she pay for her visit?" she asked, curious. The last hour had been one of the strangest in her entire career. The universe had suddenly and inexplicitly turned itself upside down and she was no longer certain of anything.

"With a credit card that was issued to God. I guess it's some sort of corporation," she replied.

Helen laughed. "I suppose they specialize in inspirational products."

"Funny, that's what she said." Carmen shrugged, and then she went back to her typing, leaving Helen to muse on her own about what all this meant.

Chapter Five

Gigi sat on the couch looking intently into the eyes of the Buddha statue while she waited for Dr. Kohlrabi, who appeared to have gone missing for a moment. This was very unlike her, but Gigi didn't mind because it afforded her the opportunity to re-examine all the trinkets that were placed throughout the office. Most of the objects were of religious origin. Gigi had yet to figure out why an agnostic Jew was so fascinated with other religions, considering she had little apparent interest in the profundity of her own. Gigi's mother had collected religious artifacts, including shrines, but her Catholicism was never a question.

"I'm sorry," Dr. Kolhrabi said, entering the room and looking rather flustered.

"What happened to your hand?" Gigi asked, noting the taped-up piece of Kleenex on Dr. Kohlrabi's palm. She'd just had a man-icure, Gigi saw. Too bad.

"I must have gotten a paper cut or something, and it appears we don't have a First Aid kit in the office. I intend to remedy that situation." She took a seat behind her desk and got her notepad out.

"That's kind of an odd place for a paper cut."

"Yes, well, what's going on with you?"

Gigi sensed Dr. Kohlrabi wasn't telling her the truth but she let it go. Not being the most forthright person herself, who was she to judge a white lie on the good doctor's part?

She said, "I've been playing racquetball with Mallory." Gigi had purposefully neglected to make mention of this before. She didn't think Dr. Kohlrabi would approve.

Dr. Kohlrabi raised an eyebrow.

"She kicked my ass. I don't have very good hand-eye coordination. It's still fun, though."

"Interesting."

"I've started working out so I'll be better competition. I don't want her to get bored with me. Caroline thinks I've gone nutty. Why are people so suspicious of change?"

"Because wild mood swings and quick changes in behavior usually indicate unsound states of mind. You probably came home with a highly elated mood and now you have a new habit."

Gigi chortled. "Like I was ever sound to begin with."

"Doesn't Caroline have a right to be suspicious?"

"What do you mean?"

"Aren't you doing all this and feeling this way because of Mallory?"

"Well, I guess so."

"Guess so?" Dr. Kohlrabi repeated.

"All right, yes. Mallory has always been the one constant in my life. I can't tell a story or think of anything in the past that doesn't include her. Without her, it seems like half my life is missing."

"My concern here is that you're back to your clandestine ways and probably dragging Mallory into it with you. This is not a good idea for either one of you."

"So if I come clean and tell Caroline that would make it all right?"

"Mending fences, as long as it's done without injuring others, is perfectly acceptable and perhaps even admirable." Dr. Kohlrabi stared at her with those impenetrable brown eyes.

"I get it. Being upstanding is almost as complex as hiding things." Gigi pulled her shorts down. She needed to start wearing longer shorts so her legs wouldn't stick to the leather couch. Plus her feet were sweating in the rubber rain boots she was wearing. She noticed Dr. Kohlrabi look at her unusual choice of footwear but she didn't say anything. Gigi didn't want to talk about it anyway.

"It can be. I want you to be serious about this. Mallory has come a long way and mostly without you. It's now up to you not to do anything that will hurt her in the future. Do I have your word?"

"I swear to God."

"Next week then?"

"Yes. Your hand is still bleeding." Gigi stood up to leave.

"I know."

Gigi paused, feeling suddenly contrite. "You know, I want to do this right."

"You are improving."

"You shouldn't tell me that." Gigi shook her head.

"Why not?" Dr. Kohlrabi said. She wadded up another Kleenex and held it to her palm.

"Because then I'll start to slack off again."

"I'm not so sure. I think you've gone too far now."

"You mean being decent could become a permanent state of mind."

"Stranger things have happened." Dr. Kohlrabi smiled.

Gigi smiled. "I'll see you next week."

Gigi opened the door to find God in the waiting room. "What are you doing here?" she screeched.

"Same thing you are, although usually I have my appointments in the morning, but today I had something else to do," God said rather matter-of-factly.

"You know each other and you didn't tell me," Gigi said, glancing back at Dr. Kohlrabi, who was still seated at her desk.

"Patient-doctor confidentiality," Dr. Kohlrabi replied. She had gotten up from behind her desk and walked toward Gigi.

"You can't keep popping up like this," Gigi said to God.

"Don't tell me what to do, you little pipsqueak," God said, walking into the office and taking a seat on the couch.

"I don't see why you need therapy," Gigi said.

"Higher beings have needs too. Besides, I don't know why I'm explaining things to you anyway. You're always raining on my parade."

"I am not."

"First the potluck and now this," God countered. A small thunderbolt exited God's forefinger and suddenly the sprinkler system began flooding the reception area.

"Are we going to behave?"

Gigi was soaked. "Yes."

"Promise?" God asked.

Gigi looked at Dr. Kohlrabi, who said nothing. She wasn't wet at all. "Yes, I promise."

"All right then," God said.

"I'll be right there." Dr. Kohlrabi escorted Gigi to the door. There was a half-inch of water in the center of the waiting room.

"Now do you understand my life?" Gigi said once God was out of earshot.

"Yes and no. Perhaps, you shouldn't argue with the Almighty. I get it about the rubber boots now."

"I'm not trying to be antagonistic."

"What happened here?" Carmen said, as she came around the corner from the ladies' room.

"The sprinkler system must have malfunctioned," Dr. Kohlrabi said, giving Gigi a pregnant look.

"Yeah, I was just standing here and next thing I knew the thing just drenched me."

"I'll call maintenance," Carmen said, picking up the phone.

"Tell them we need a mop," Dr. Kohlrabi suggested.

Later that evening, Gigi came in the house dripping with sweat. She flopped down on the weight bench, which had now become a permanent fixture in the middle of the living room. Caroline looked up from her computer as Gigi mimicked the exercises from the chart she had hanging on the wall.

"What's with the exercise craze?"

"It's part of the new me," Gigi replied. She wiped her face on the towel hanging on the weight bench.

"You should really wash that."

Gigi gave it a sniff. "You're right. It smells disgusting."

Caroline followed her to the kitchen where she downed a protein shake from a can she had cooling in the fridge. It was the only way she could drink them.

"This stuff is disgusting," Gigi said, wincing.

"Then why are you drinking it?"

"Because Mallory won't play racquetball with me if I don't have some stamina." Gigi shrugged.

"So that's what all this is about," Caroline said.

Gigi saw the color rise in Caroline's face and she knew she was in trouble. "I'm sure working out has other benefits. I've never really tried it before," Gigi replied, squeezing her bicep.

"How long have you been seeing Mallory?"

"For a while," Gigi said, hedging. "I saw her at the flower shop and then we started playing racquetball on Thursdays."

"That's all?"

"Well, yeah."

Suddenly Caroline hit her hard in the arm and screamed, "I don't understand you, her, this or us!" She slammed the door before Gigi had a chance to respond.

❧

"I think I understand why clandestine is better," Gigi told Mallory the next time they played. Caroline hadn't spoken to her for a week.

"No, upfront is better but you have to have some social skills," Mallory said. She served the ball hard. "And unfortunately, you have the social skills of a moron."

"I am not a moron," Gigi said, glaring at her. The ball bounced off the corner and hit her square in the forehead. A seething pain ran behind Gigi's eyes. She never saw it coming. "Damn!" She rubbed her forehead.

Mallory laughed and when she had composed herself enough she asked, "Are you all right?"

"Not exactly. First you insult my dignity and then my body."

Mallory came over to inspect the perfectly round welt in the center of Gigi's forehead. "Wow, I really nailed you. It was an accident and you should have been watching the ball."

"Gee, that makes me feel better."

"I'm sorry. It's really hard to have such a killer serve and have a moron for a partner."

"I can't believe how much better you're making me feel. Now, since you're so fucking smart, what did I do wrong and why is Caroline so mad at me?"

"You told her in an off-hand way. You should have discussed it with her and perhaps asked her advice."

"All that?" Gigi studied Mallory's face. Sometimes she forgot how pretty she was with her long blonde, curly hair and deep blue eyes. Gigi had been in love with Mallory since they were ten and they'd met in Brownies. Unfortunately, she'd never had the courage to do anything about it . . . except sleeping with her girlfriend. Sometimes she could convince herself that she'd done it to be closer to Mallory, but that didn't explain why she loved Caroline. It was an endless source of confusion. Still, it felt good to have Mallory around.

"If you want to stay out of trouble."

"This seems like a lot of work. Maybe I should have just kept my mouth shut."

"That's what always gets you in trouble, remember?"

"Yes."

"Now, can we play? And for shit's sake keep your eye on the ball."

"Have you told Del yet?"

"No," Mallory said, getting ready to serve.

"Ah-hah!"

"I plan on telling her. I didn't want to bother her about it unless I decided that we were going to keep on playing together."

"Can we be friends again?" Gigi asked, her eyes getting misty.

"Only if you promise to behave yourself and never, ever lie to me again. Do you realize how much of my life I wasted pining over Caroline when if you had only told me that she loved you and not me I could have moved on. Not to mention the therapy bills."

"I think the therapy did you good."

Mallory served the ball hard again.

"I promise to be good. Besides, you never would have met Del." Gigi completely missed the ball.

"And you have to work on your swing."

"I will."

"You know, my only vindication for this whole thing is that you and Caroline are now finally together and can torture each other on a daily basis. Life is good." Mallory served the ball again.

"You used to be a lot sweeter." Gigi hit the ball this time.

"Ignorance is bliss." Mallory hit it back hard.

"I still love you and you have great legs."

"Then learn to play better."

When Caroline got home from work Friday evening, Gigi had cleaned the house and the table was set for dinner. She came into the dining room carrying a vase of brilliant white daisies, which she placed in the center of the dining room table. She'd finally thrown out the calla lilies, which had become practically petrified. She looked at Caroline sheepishly.

"This looks nice," Caroline said diplomatically.

"I'm sorry about Mallory. I should have told you earlier and as Mallory put it, I have the social skills of a moron. I guess she's right."

Caroline laughed. "Boy, you can say that again. What happened to your forehead?"

"I was too busy being insulted to pay attention to the whereabouts of the ball."

"And you got cold-cocked."

"I supposed it was payback in the karmic sense."

Caroline came closer. She ran her forefinger across the bump. "Does it still hurt?"

"A little," Gigi said, her face getting hot. Even though they lived together, close proximity always gave her a charge and made her nervous at the same time. It was always this way with Caroline. It was what had first drawn her to Caroline, the stew of emotions she felt any time they got close. Gigi felt Caroline drawing her closer. She ran her hand down Caroline's back until their bodies touched completely. Gigi nuzzled her neck.

Caroline lifted her chin and gazed in her eyes. "I have missed you." And then she kissed her.

"Is this okay?" Gigi asked.

"Oh, Gigi."

They kissed again and Gigi couldn't decide if she should mention dinner or suggest the bedroom. This was a big step and she was scared shitless. In the end, it was Caroline who made the decision.

"We should stop or I'm going to need a cold shower."

"Or we could keep going and take it somewhere soft and cuddly," Gigi said, nibbling Caroline's shoulder. It was supposed to be romantic but all Gigi got was a mouthful of T-shirt. Real life was never like the lesbian novels.

"Are you sure you're ready for that? Gigi, I can't go to that place if you're going to bail on me again."

Gigi studied her face. "I'm ready to stop playing this game. I want to make love. I want to behave like a couple and I want to get on with our lives. If that's all right with you."

Caroline was quiet for a moment. Gigi could feel her heart begin to pound as if the weight of her whole life were being decided at this moment. Caroline took her hand and led her to the bedroom.

"Does this mean yes?"

Caroline pinched her hard.

"Remember, my social skills aren't that good."

"I intend to remedy that," Caroline said. She pulled Gigi's T-shirt off.

"What? Are you going to send me to charm school?"

"You could certainly use it."

"Maybe you could teach me," Gigi said. She watched as Caroline took off her shirt and then her shorts. Suddenly, she didn't feel like talking anymore.

Gigi set her down gently on the bed. Caroline kissed her softly. Gigi slid off her own shorts and undid her bra. Then she eased Caroline back on the bed. She kissed Caroline's nipple and then traced the outline of her breast with her tongue.

"I had forgotten how beautiful your breasts are," Gigi said, slowly running her tongue around the smooth pink nipple again.

"They, on the other hand, have never forgotten you," Caroline said.

"Hmm . . ." Gigi said. "How kind of them."

Caroline's breath grew ragged as Gigi kissed her stomach and flicked her tongue down one thigh and up the other. She opened her legs wider and Gigi ran her tongue between Caroline's now very wet lips, flicking softly at first and then harder against her clitoris. Gigi had to concentrate on not coming. She wanted to wait for Caroline but it had been so long since she'd had this feeling, and at one point she wasn't certain she was ever going to feel like having sex again. Everything had gone so badly and it all appeared linked to getting off. But this was love, Gigi told herself. This was different. She felt Caroline come.

Then Caroline, who must have sensed that Gigi was already almost there, rolled her on her stomach and entered her from behind. First one finger, then two and finally three. Gigi thrust hard against her until she couldn't contain her orgasm a second longer. Gigi let out a long groan. She rolled back over. "That was nice."

"So nice." Caroline took a deep breath.

"I'm thinking abstinence does make the heart grow stronger."

"It's absence that makes the heart grow fonder," Caroline corrected her.

"I like my version better," Gigi said, pulling Caroline back on top of her. She smiled as she ran her hand between Caroline's thighs.

Caroline pulled Gigi toward her and they rocked against each other until they both came within seconds of each other. They both flopped back down on the bed.

Gigi gazed into Caroline's eyes. "Why did this take so long?"

"Because you were a coward," Caroline said, taking Gigi's hand and placing it between her thighs. "Tonight, let's make up for all the lost time and then we can start over."

Gigi sighed. "That sounds wonderful."

It was midnight when Gigi got up to go pee and get a drink of water. She had carefully unraveled herself from the love knot she had formed with Caroline. The last candle flickered out as Gigi gazed down at Caroline. She was a beautiful woman and Gigi swore she would treat her better. She pulled the sheet up over Caroline's naked shoulders. The night had finally cooled off. She turned off the fan and crept out of the room.

Gigi found God in the dining room eating the chocolate mousse Gigi had purchased for dessert.

"This is good," God said around a mouthful of mousse. She patted a chair next to her at the table.

Gigi sat down. "That was supposed to be for after dinner tonight."

"Yes, it seems you didn't get as far as dinner. May I suggest steak and eggs for your lovebird's breakfast. You'll really score major points with that one."

"Good idea. Wait a minute . . . you know about tonight?"

"I'm omniscient, remember."

"You didn't watch, did you?" Gigi tried hard not to imagine God watching her scraggly ass banging against Caroline. She winced at the very thought of it.

"Of course not," God replied indignantly.

"You didn't make that happen."

"No, sweetie darling, you did that all on your own. I may have invented orgasms but I don't create them."

"Why did you do that?" Gigi asked, suddenly curious why her body was wired in such a way. Looking at God eating suddenly reminded Gigi how hungry she was. She got herself a bowl and had some mousse. It was delicious.

"Do what?" God scooped the rest of the mousse out of the bowl, scraping the bottom with her spoon. "Damn, that stuff's good."

"Create orgasms."

"Oh, that. Well, I needed an impetus to get you people to breed. I wanted you to have fun doing it. Sex is kind of weird when you think about it. I was concerned that humans, being as smart as they are, would see this. I needed to come up with an incentive." God stuffed her face close to the daisies that were on the table. "Daisies don't really have a smell. I don't know what it should be but they should have something."

"They're some new weird kind of genetically engineered

68

flower. I wanted daffodils but the florist said they're out of season already."

"Now that we have that settled, there's another thing I'd like to discuss with you."

"You mean orgasms and flowers?" Gigi liked to clarify. Not understanding God correctly could have dire consequences.

"Yes."

"All right." Gigi folded her hands on the table and did her best to pay attention. She was suddenly exhausted and this wasn't what she had planned for the evening. Caroline's warm body was waiting for her and she wanted to get back there and run her hand down Caroline's lean torso and maybe somewhere else.

"My goodness, my little heathen has come a long way since we first met. Remember when we talked about my having a plan for you?"

Gigi gulped. "Now's the time?"

"Yes."

"What do I have to do?" Gigi asked, suddenly wide awake, her mind racing through a series of awful scenarios, all of which involved pain and ridicule.

"I want you to write a self-help book for me."

Gigi nearly fell off her chair she was laughing so hard.

"Shh! You'll wake her up." God got up from the dining room table and stood at the edge of the hallway. She listened intently. The bedroom door was wide open. Caroline groaned from the bedroom and then was quiet again.

Gigi clamped her mouth shut but she couldn't stop laughing. She heard on the radio that someone had died trying to contain a sneeze. She hoped the same wasn't true for laughing.

"What is so funny?" God asked indignantly. She went to the couch and brought over a black briefcase like a businessman would carry.

"Have you lost your mind?" Gigi looked askance at the bag.

"No, I am in full control of all my faculties—in fact, I feel extremely focused."

"Why in the hell do you want to write a self-help book? We've got a million of them out there already, and as you can see by the wretched state of the place, they haven't done any good."

"I'm not ready to give up yet. This one will be different."

Gigi wiped her eyes. "You're just like a hopeful parent who keeps thinking that one day their rotten kid will morph into some amazingly decent person. Don't count on it. In my opinion, human beings are basically rotten."

"You're so pessimistic. There's good in some of you. So humor me."

"I don't know how to write."

"You will. I'll teach you. See that stack of books over there? You'll read those and I'll dictate the book to you while you bone up on the particulars," God said, pointing to the laptop she pulled out of the mysterious briefcase.

"Why do I have to study the books?"

"Because an idiot can't write a masterpiece. You'll need some credibility."

"I was never a good student." Gigi eyed the stack of books. It looked like a lot of work.

"You will be now."

"Or?"

"Trust me, you won't like the consequences."

Gigi imagined the errant sprinkler system going off at work, at the racquetball court, in the grocery store. "I've become suddenly very motivated."

"Great! Now let's get started." God flipped open the laptop and looked at her. "I assume you know how to use one of these."

"Unfortunately, yes." Gigi knew for certain that God was serious about this book thing. She supposed this was better than some of the other scenarios she had imagined. Anything to do with God was not going to be easy, but she guessed if she could get her body strong for Mallory, she could exercise her mind a little for the Almighty. This notion of not being selfish anymore was really kind of a drag. She pulled the laptop toward her. "What do you want to call it?" She looked inquiringly at God, who was standing up and seemed engrossed in thought. Oh, great, Gigi thought, she's in a writer's trance.

"*The Philosophy of Water.*"

"Interesting title," Gigi mumbled.

The next morning Gigi was slumped over her computer when she felt a gentle touch on her shoulder.

"Gigi, are you all right?"

"I'm tired! I can't do any more," Gigi said, sitting up and blinking. "Oh, it's you. Good morning. Is it still Saturday?" The last time she spent that much time with God she slept through an entire weekend.

"Yes, it's still Saturday. Who were you talking to?"

"God. She's a slave-driver," Gigi said, taking a good look around.

"There's no one here."

"Oh, good."

"What are you doing?" Caroline asked, pointing to the computer. "And where'd you get that?"

"I'm writing a book and I picked that up yesterday." Gigi figured it wasn't exactly a lie.

"I didn't know you were a writer."

Gigi could tell from the tone of her voice that Caroline thought she was completely nuts. She was capable of certain things but a literary genius she was not. "I'm not."

"Well, you're on page twenty-seven. Can I read it?"

"I suppose so," Gigi said, looking around. "There's no thunderbolts so I guess we're all right." Gigi got up and offered Caroline the chair. "Hey, you want steak and eggs for breakfast since we never got around to dinner?"

"Sure, that's sounds wonderful," Caroline said, scrolling back to the beginning of the book.

Gigi went to make breakfast. She started the coffee and then cut up some green onions and tomatoes for omelets. She was humming to herself when Caroline found her out back on the patio. It was still early so the scorching heat of the summer day had not yet begun. There was a slight breeze that rustled the queen palm next to the pool. The sky was a perfect blue and for once in a long time, Gigi felt genuinely happy.

"You know, I really enjoy cooking when I have someone to cook for," Gigi said, giving her a big hug.

"Your book is really good."

"It is?" Gigi said, putting the steaks on the grill.

"Yes, I had no idea you were so intuitive."

"I'm not," Gigi said. She opened the arcadia door and went into the kitchen. Caroline followed her.

"But you wrote that."

"Not really." Gigi got the eggs out of the fridge and cracked them in a bowl. She was hoping this would distract Caroline from the book tangent. Gigi really didn't want to get into it. People were going to be amazed that she knew enough English grammar to write a correct paragraph. How would they react to a book? Perhaps God should have chosen someone more qualified.

"How can you not really write a book?"

"I'm telling you. I didn't write it. I'm just the ghostwriter or whatever those people are called who write about what someone tells them."

"Whose book is it then?"

"God is actually the one writing it." Gigi got a pan out of the cupboard and started the eggs.

"Have you been talking to your mother again?"

"No, she still hates me."

"Well, whoever is typing those words into the computer should keep it up."

"I don't think I have a choice. I can only imagine what defiance would bring," Gigi muttered.

The steak and omelets were delicious, and Gigi and Caroline spent the rest of the weekend in each other's arms and eating. Gigi decided these were her two favorite pastimes. God left her alone for the next couple of days, although Gigi kept looking over her shoulder waiting for an appearance.

The following Thursday afternoon, Mallory was poking around in Gigi's book bag. "What on earth is going on here?" Mallory asked. "I mean, you've got books on religion, philosophy, spirituality, psychology and history. I didn't think you knew how to read."

Gigi scowled at her. "I know how to read. I just don't like to read, but I have to study them or else."

"Why? Are you back in summer school or something?" Mallory said, stuffing them back into the bag.

"Because I need credibility and in my current state of idiocy I had better get cracking."

"Gigi, what is going on?"

"I'll tell you when I pull it off." Gigi sat down on the locker room bench and changed into her tennis shoes. She pulled the racquet out of her bag and began straightening out the strings and doing her best to avoid Mallory's gaze.

"Gigi, no more secrets. I mean it or I'm out of here," Mallory said, her hands on her hips and a determined look on her face.

"All right. This is not about a woman. I actually might just grow up to be a good partner," Gigi said, thinking back to having breakfast with Caroline that morning and then having Caroline. Caroline was teaching a night class and Gigi didn't have to go to work until ten. She had made Caroline toast and strawberries and brought them to her in bed.

"Then what it is?" Mallory demanded.

Gigi could see the scar on Mallory's forearm. She had caused that. Mallory had walked through the closed sliding glass door

73

after she had found out that Gigi and Caroline had had an affair. Gigi never really understood why Caroline had taken a shine to her. Mallory had long blonde, slightly wavy hair and blue eyes. She was slim with very nice breasts and one of those nicely shaped hind ends. She was gorgeous by anyone's standards. Why Caroline wrecked her relationship with Mallory, who adored her, was still beyond her comprehension, unless Caroline was a glutton for punishment. Gigi winced and confessed, "I'm writing a self-help book."

Mallory started laughing so hard she was bent double, wiping tears out of her eyes.

"You look like you're having a seizure. What's so funny?" Gigi picked one of the books out of the bag and studied the title, *Classics of Western Thought*. This was possible; lesser beings than herself had done good things. Certainly she was capable of doing something. Besides, she was going to have help.

"It's just that you are, shall we say, not the most academically inclined person I've ever known. I mean, if you hadn't been banging the math teacher in high school you never would have graduated." Mallory sat back down on the bench and wiped her eyes with the hem of her T-shirt.

"My past performance is not necessarily indicative of my future performance. I can do this!" Gigi thrust the book back in her bag and stomped off.

"Hey, where are you going? I thought we were going to play racquetball."

"To the library. I have to study."

"Come on. Let's play and then I'll go with you and help," Mallory offered.

"You promise not to make fun of me anymore?"

"I promise. Look, if you want to improve yourself, I'm all for it."

"Thank you. All right, let's go play. Have you told Del about us yet?"

"Yes," Mallory said, getting the racquet out of her locker.

"What did she say?"

"That she would kill you with her bare hands if you do anything to hurt me."

"I'm glad she's taking it so well," Gigi said. She was trying to stuff her book bag into her locker and it wasn't working.

"Maybe you shouldn't carry so many books around at one time," Mallory suggested as she went to help.

"It's part of the training."

Gigi was on her lunch break the next day at the photography studio. She was eating an apple, having discovered the amazing land of fruit. It wasn't the foreign stuff she had once viewed it as. She was forgoing Twinkies in lieu of healthier foods. She was reading a book on great Eastern philosophers. So far Gandhi was her favorite. She hoped God wasn't entertaining any ideas about having her run around with a sheet wrapped around her private parts spouting platitudes of peace, love and understanding. For one thing, her skinny legs would look horrible sticking out of an oversized diaper. She kept telling herself it was all academic. Gigi looked up from her reading when her boss walked into the room.

"Gigi, have you seen these proofs?"

"No." Gigi took the proofs from Danielle. Each photo showed a person with iridescent colors surrounding his or her body. Each one was different. "It looks like poor developing. Did I do that?"

"No, but you took the photos. That senior class we shot Monday. I developed them. It's not the camera or the film."

"What the hell, then?"

"Have you ever seen auras?" Danielle asked.

"No, what are auras?"

"They're the energy that surrounds our bodies. We all have a different ones; each one is unique. That's what these are photographs of."

"Does this mean my career as a photographer is finished?" Gigi suddenly grasped where this was going. Obviously, hanging out with God was starting to have repercussions. Now she took pictures of people surrounded by weird colors and then there was the thing with her feet. The inside of her arches were starting to peel and despite various lotions nothing seemed to work. Caroline had done some research on the Internet and was concocting strange-smelling poultices that she wrapped around Gigi's feet. She took her shoe off and vigorously scratched the bottom of her foot.

"Not necessarily. I was thinking that we might branch out a bit."

"What do you mean?"

"Having you take pictures of people's auras. It's all that New Age stuff. Let's give it a try."

"So I still have a job?"

"Of course, and you might even get a raise if this thing works out," Danielle said. She winked at Gigi. She handed Gigi her camera. "Now, I want you to take one of me."

"Sure."

They went to the studio and Gigi started her new career as a New Age photographer. She couldn't help thinking there might be consequences to this as well. What if people didn't like the color that their auras came in? She'd have to ask God why everything good seemed to have a downside and vice versa. Was it some sort of cosmic joke?

Danielle sat down and Gigi took the shot. "What if you don't like your colors?"

"I'll fire you."

Gigi was mortified.

"I was just kidding, relax."

Gigi smiled and began setting up the next shot.

Chapter Six

On Monday evening just after seven, Helen waited patiently for her daughter at the Chez Nous restaurant. It was a French bistro around the corner from Megan's office. The floor was tiled in black and white and the tables were painted various colors. Helen liked French things. She had spent a semester in college in Paris and loved it. She took a sip of wine and glanced at the clock on the wall. Megan was late. She was usually so punctual, Helen thought, unless she got held up in court. She wondered if she had come to her senses about Jeff. One human being shouldn't leave another out to dry. As a therapist's daughter, Megan should know better.

Just then Megan came flying into the restaurant, located her mother and then plopped down in the chair across from her. "Wow, sorry I'm late."

"Court?"

"Exactly, and you know how everything goes wrong when

you're running late." Megan poured herself a glass of the water from the carafe on the table.

"You looked stressed," Helen said, taking her daughter's chin and turning her face toward her. Megan winced. "What happened to your face?"

"It's not that bad."

"Did he do that?" Helen asked, praying that Jeff had not turned into some kind of stalker. Megan had told her that he'd been calling a lot and Helen had been worried ever since.

"Who are you talking about?"

"Jeff, the man you were going to marry."

"No," Megan replied. She took a sip of water.

"So what happened to your face?" Helen said, looking at it again. Megan had a scrape that ran the length of her chin.

Megan pulled away. "It's really all right." She signaled the waiter. "Can I get a martini with olives?"

"Certainly," the waiter replied. "Anything for you, ma'am?"

"No, I'm fine, thank you." When he had left, Helen said, "So you were saying?" She wasn't going to let her off the hook. She wanted to know what was going on and she wouldn't rest until she knew.

"I fell off my bike at South Mountain this past weekend."

The waiter returned with Megan's drink, and Helen asked for a few more minutes with the menu.

"I didn't know you mountain-biked."

"It's a new sport." Megan sipped her martini and looked out the window.

"Like the fishing thing." Helen could tell Megan was avoiding her. She had discovered over the course of their mother-daughter relationship that Megan tended to downplay things, places or people that were becoming important to her, as if she were afraid that by sharing them they would somehow be spoiled or taken away from her. Helen thought it might be tied to Lars' leaving them.

"Correct," Megan said, picking up a menu and perusing its contents.

"So who's opening up all these new vistas for you?"

"Mother, if I didn't know better I'd think you were analyzing me."

Helen studied her daughter's face. Megan looked a lot like her. She had shoulder-length blonde hair that was streaked almost white in places from the sun, and she had her father's blue eyes and full lips. She had Helen's slim nose. She was a very pretty young woman and that had always made Helen nervous. When Megan was a child people commented on how pretty she was, Helen would downplay it so Megan grew up not focusing on her looks. This made her all the more appealing. "I would never. I'm simply exhibiting the normal amount of motherly concern over a daughter who happens to be experiencing some unusual life changes, that's all." Helen flipped open her menu in order to distract Megan from pursuing this line of questioning.

"Life changes?"

"Well, you're behaving differently and you have a new friend."

"Yes, I suppose you're right." Megan surveyed the menu. "What are you going to have?"

"Soup du jour and the stuffed crab croissant. So who is he?" Helen continued to study the menu, which was absurd because she'd already decided.

"It's not a he, it's a woman from work. Her name is Rafferty and she's the boss's daughter."

"I see," Helen said, closing her menu. "Girl time is good." She was secretly relieved. Helen didn't want Megan rushing into anything while she was still rebounding. "So you really like Rafferty?"

"Yes. I like being with her. She's quirky and smart and, I don't know, exciting. Jeff was not exciting."

The waiter brought them bread and cheese and then replaced the water carafe. Helen ordered another glass of wine.

"Newness is always exciting."

"I know, but how do you really know if it's love? I walked out of Jeff's life and after two weeks I've stopped thinking about him. And I was going to get married. That scares me."

"It is possible that Jeff was in love with you and you were in love with the concept of being loved. Does that make sense?"

"Not really."

"What I mean is, being loved and adored is a heady thing and it creates an infatuation that can parade as love, then something changes and you start to see the person for who they are," Helen explained.

"And what you thought was love dissipates."

"Correct."

"Some people get married on that, don't they?"

"Yes, they do," Helen said, thinking of herself. Lars was a prick with a good sales pitch.

The waiter came to take their order.

"Have you decided?" Helen asked Megan.

"I think I'll have the same thing as you, the soup du jour and the stuffed crab croissant."

"Have you tried them before?"

"No."

"Oh, they're absolutely marvelous."

"I'll have another martini," Megan told the waiter.

Helen raised her eyebrows.

"I can still legally drive, Mom. Stop worrying, everything is fine. I'm feeling a lot better lately."

"Okay, I'll try. So tell me, how did the case work out with the American woman and her Brazilian lover? Does she get to stay?"

"Yes, but they have to move to Vermont."

"Vermont?"

"Yes, they can legally wed there and then the Brazilian can apply for citizenship. It's not really a win, more like a circumlocution. Rafferty thinks it's a cop-out. She's gay, you know, so she takes the civil rights thing really seriously."

"And you just like to win the case."

Megan smiled. "Well, of course."

When their order arrived Megan ate with a relish. Helen breathed a sigh of relief. She always felt better when Megan came clean. It just took her a while. Her daughter had always been her toughest patient.

"This is marvelous," Megan said after she'd taken her third bite of crab.

"I thought you'd like it."

"I'll have to bring Rafferty here. She'd love it."

"So does Rafferty have a girlfriend?"

"Mom!"

"I know, I'm prying again." Helen had her soup and told herself to relax.

The next day during the staff meeting, Megan noticed Bel eyeing her cut chin. It was nearly healed, and Megan had taken great pains to use a clear Band-Aid. Still, it was apparent she'd done something to her face and it wasn't a pimple. Rafferty's band-aged elbow only added to Bel's consternation. Megan saw her tuck her arm under the table to keep it hidden. Rafferty had tripped over a rock when she came running to see if Megan was all right after she flipped over the handlebars of her bike. Rafferty was an avid mountain biker and she wanted to share her passion with Megan, telling her it was a total rush. Rafferty had several bikes so she lent one to Megan, who took to it the same way she took to fishing, with excitement and enthusiasm. She just wished she wasn't so klutzy. Bel had taken a long weekend to go with Harold to Palm Springs so she had been off on Monday. Megan knew it was just a matter of time before they were to be interrogated.

Bel maintained her composure until she was through doling out the week's assignments. At the end of the meeting she held them back. "Rafferty and Megan, a word, please."

Megan and Rafferty exchanged looks. This was a good thing or a bad thing. Megan figured on the latter.

Bel shut the door behind them. "I want you two to stop this daredevil fourteen-year-old-boy behavior. I don't need my two best lawyers in body casts. Is that understood?"

Megan could tell Rafferty was about to say something along the lines of "Mind your own business," but she gave her a stern look that stopped her before Rafferty got into a full-fledged argument with Bel.

"Yes, ma'am," they both echoed in unison.

Bel opened the door and said, "By the way, I took the liberty of canceling your skydiving lessons for next weekend and purchased you symphony tickets instead."

Megan wondered how she'd found out about the lessons.

"I hate the symphony," Rafferty whined.

"In that case, I'll use them and take Harold. Have a nice rest of the day, ladies."

"So, now what are we going to do this weekend?" Rafferty asked.

"How about a hot tub, a steak and lobster dinner and a really cheesy chick flick with lots of cold beer," Megan suggested. "After you go to the chiropractor and get your neck fixed."

"At least she didn't find out about the rock gym."

"It was my fault I dropped you. I can still see the safety line flying through my hands and being helpless to stop it. I am so sorry." They were taking rock-climbing lessons at the rock gym. It had been Megan's idea. Everyone had a partner and the instructor had been just as mortified as Megan when Rafferty flopped down on the padded mat in front of the climbing structure. Luckily she hadn't been that high on the wall.

"I'm fine. It's just a little kinked, that's all."

"So what about dinner?"

Rafferty smiled. "Only if we can go hiking on Saturday morning and I can get skinned knees or something. She has no right to tell us what we can and cannot do outside of work."

"But she does have the power to give us all the shit cases. Retribution sucks."

"Sometimes I hate working for my mother."

"I know. Hey, I went to this great French bistro with my mom last night. Want to go there for lunch?" Megan was trying to distract her. Rafferty, she knew, was going to obsess about this episode for the rest of the week until she could defy her mother on Saturday. Until then, Megan was going to have to keep her busy.

"What time?"

"How about one?"

"Can we make it about one-thirty. I have a little midmorning errand to run."

"Are you going to that place where you get your shoes all dirty?"

"Something like that."

"Are you going to tell me about these little disappearing acts of yours someday?"

"Perhaps."

It seemed an eternity before the weekend came. Rafferty had been crabby most of the week. Megan got everything prepped before Rafferty arrived. She had snuck out of work early so she could shop and have a chance to clean up. She had purchased a dozen multicolored sunflowers for the dining room table but she had abstained from candles. She thought those might be too overt. She was quite aware of her intentions for the evening but she was pretty sure Rafferty didn't have a clue.

Megan had been grappling with her feelings ever since the fishing trip. She decided that she had fallen in love that day on the bank of the stream and this time it wasn't infatuation with someone else's love of her. It was her own private love. She didn't know exactly how one went from being straight to being gay, but she was pretty sure that you fell in love with someone of the same sex and you dealt with the polemics later. In the case with the American woman and the Brazilian woman, the American had been straight and fallen hard for her about-to-be deported lover. Megan had asked her about that and the American told her that one day it didn't matter anymore what people thought. She loved this woman and consequences be damned. Megan admired her courage.

Although Megan had never been with another woman, she was one and she felt that qualified her as knowing enough. She knew what she liked in bed, so how hard could it be to make another woman feel good. She wanted Rafferty—as a friend but also as a lover. She wanted the sensation of holding Rafferty, of being inside her, of making her quiver with delight. The doorbell rang and broke her train of thought.

"It smells wonderful in here," Rafferty said. "And the flowers are a nice addition. We should have candles."

"I've got some," Megan said.

"How fortuitous," Rafferty said. "I guess this isn't such a bad substitute for skydiving."

Megan could tell she was still angry about her mother's meddling, but they had made an appointment to go up in a glider the following weekend and that had helped Rafferty's mood. "Thanks." Megan pulled two Coronas out of the fridge. She cut up a lime while Rafferty inspected the big pot where the lobsters were boiling. "Don't look."

"Why not?" Rafferty was waving her hand to disperse the steam.

"Because it's cruel. I can barely get myself to do it."

"It's part of the food chain." Rafferty put the lid back on. "Oh, my God, I can hear them screaming."

Megan pinched her arm. "Stop it."

"See, there it is again. Can't you hear them? 'Let me out of the pot. I'm melting, I'm melting.' " Rafferty did a lobster imitation, her arms flaying wildly.

"You are horrible." Megan stuffed a lime in the bottle of Corona and handed it to her.

Megan noticed the toe of Rafferty's boot was covered in horse dung. Rafferty casually sauntered out on the deck of Megan's condo. "The coals look ready. Do you want me to put the steaks on?"

"Sure," Megan said. She brought the steaks out on a plate. They were two huge porterhouse steaks.

"Those look great." Rafferty put them on the grill, first searing one side and then the other. She turned the gas down on the grill and closed the lid.

"You do that so well."

"I love barbequing." Rafferty sat down in one of the lawn chairs and nonchalantly removed her boots.

"Thanks for coming," Megan said as she leaned over and gently squeezed Rafferty's thigh. "So you've been to the barn, I see."

"What are you talking about?"

Megan pointed to Rafferty's boot. "You've got horse shit on them. There's only a few places where one can get that and it's not in the city."

"It's just this place I go to. It helps me relax."

"Maybe we could go there someday. When you're ready," Megan said gently.

"Someday I will. You know, I like spending time with you." Rafferty took her socks off but avoided meeting Megan's gaze.

"But I impinge on your love life."

Rafferty took a sip of beer and looked at Megan quizzically. "What do you mean?"

"You spend all your time with me."

"And you keep me from doing damage to my heart by dating worthless causes. I have never felt better than I do now. So stop worrying. I better check the steaks." Rafferty hopped up.

Megan could tell she was getting nervous.

Rafferty pulled the steaks off. "So how is your love life lately?"

"It's wonderful."

"Who are you seeing?" Rafferty asked. She appeared shocked.

"Like you don't know." Megan took the steaks inside and Rafferty followed her.

"I don't. Who are you seeing?"

"You, silly," Megan said. She put the steaks on the counter. Megan stroked the side of Rafferty's face. Rafferty was saved from further embarrassment by the kitchen timer going off and Megan inwardly cursed. This would have been the perfect time to kiss Rafferty but the lobsters were ready. Rafferty was blushing so Megan pinched her arm. This was going to be a little more difficult than she imagined. Rafferty, it appeared, was not going to be much help. "Don't worry, you don't have to marry me anytime soon."

"You're messing with me," Rafferty said. She was no longer blushing so she appeared to have collected herself.

"No, I'm serious."

"About what?"

"Getting in bed with you."

Rafferty tried to laugh. "Yeah, right."

"Wait and see. Now let's eat before everything gets cold."

After they had cleared away the dishes, Rafferty stood in the kitchen rubbing her tummy. "Dinner was fabulous."

"I think my culinary skills are improving."

"Thank you," Rafferty said, pouring them each another glass of wine. "You'll make someone an awesome partner someday."

"So will you," Megan said, starting the dishwater and immersing the pans.

"I'll do the dishes," Rafferty offered.

Megan turned around, thinking it was now or never. "Rafferty, can I kiss you?"

"What?"

Before Rafferty could protest Megan had her up against the sink and was ardently kissing her. Megan felt Rafferty's tongue dancing and twisting with her own, which was offering no protest. Megan pulled her closer and kissed her neck. Megan knew Rafferty was totally succumbing to the moment and this was a good thing.

"You don't know how long I've wanted to do that," Megan said, reaching for Rafferty's breast, her fingertips tracing the outline of her nipple.

Rafferty eyes were panicked. "This isn't good."

Megan kissed her forehead, her eyelids and then her lips. "No, this is really good."

"Megan, I can't do this. I just can't," she said, pulling away.

"What's wrong?"

"I've gotta go," Rafferty said. She bolted from the kitchen.

"Rafferty, wait!" She heard the door shut and tires screech out of the drive. Megan stood there in shock for a moment and then she got angry. Rafferty wasn't going to get off that easy. They were going to resolve this tonight, before Rafferty had time to build up a case against her as she knew she would. Rafferty loved her, Megan could feel it, but it was a matter of convincing her that this could work.

Megan dug around for her car keys. When she tripped over the rug in the foyer she thought better of driving. She'd had a few too many drinks to get behind the wheel. She contemplated calling a cab and then decided to walk. Both she and Rafferty lived in condos along Phoenix's central corridor. Rafferty lived exactly thirteen blocks away, on the first floor of a four-unit complex.

Halfway there the storm let loose. Thunderclouds had been building all day but most times they hung around for half a day and then moved on still holding their cargo, leaving the desert floor just as dusty and dry as when they came. But not tonight. Megan was soaked by the time she got to Rafferty's condo.

She rang the bell. She had stewed all the way there and now she was angry and wet. "You can't just leave like that!"

"I'm sorry. I freaked. Come inside, you're soaking wet."

"I'm not coming in until you tell me why you don't want me. We're perfect for each other. All I think about is you."

Rafferty was quiet for a moment. "There's just one problem. You're straight."

"Not anymore," Megan said. She started to shiver. The temperature had dropped and she was wearing only shorts and a T-shirt.

"What? You had an epiphany three seconds before you kissed me?"

"No, it's been weeks, months, years and I finally understand myself. I fall in love and you don't want me," Megan said, tears welling up in her eyes. She couldn't help it. She was crying.

Rafferty grabbed her arm and pulled her inside. "I want you. I'm scared. I don't want to fuck this up. There, I said it. Now, let's get you some dry clothes."

"You're scared. That's pretty lame." She followed Rafferty to her bedroom and began peeling off her wet clothes with the same carelessness as when they were at the gym. She was standing naked in the bedroom and she knew Rafferty still didn't have the guts to do anything about it. "Who isn't scared?" she said, continuing her diatribe. "The eco-challenged woman who is willing to throw herself out of an airplane or ride off an incline is afraid of having an argument or what? I'm not signing up for a quick fuck. I want the whole package." She stuck her hands on her hips and waited for an answer.

Rafferty just smiled.

"What?" Megan demanded.

"You're beautiful," Rafferty said, wrapping a flannel shirt around Megan's shoulders and pulling her close. She kissed her softly. "I love you."

Megan didn't know whether she could trust her. "Then show me." She pushed her toward the bed.

"What if you don't like it?" Rafferty asked as Megan unbuttoned her shirt.

Megan pushed her onto the bed. "Are you always this neurotic about sex?"

"Only with you."

"Trust me, I'll like it." She pulled off Rafferty's pants and then lowered herself down onto Rafferty, who moaned softly, then wrapped her hands around Megan's butt and pulled them together. Megan kissed her and then traced the outline of Rafferty's soft brown nipple with her tongue. She didn't know if she was supposed to be the initiator because she was technically the novice but she really didn't care. She was going to make Rafferty feel all of her. Then she flicked Rafferty's stomach with soft little kisses. Rafferty opened her legs wider and groaned. Megan kissed her inner thighs and ran her tongue between Rafferty's lips. This brought a heavy sigh from Rafferty and Megan knew she was on the right track.

Rafferty was wet. Megan ran her tongue along her clitoris and then inserted her finger. Rafferty moved against her. She pulled Megan up on top of her and reached for her. Megan was dripping when Rafferty put her fingers inside. Together they rocked against each other. Megan felt Rafferty quiver and she knew she had made her come. It was the most amazing feeling, being inside Rafferty while Rafferty was inside her. It wasn't like straight sex at all. Megan's mind finally shut down when she felt herself shudder and her whole body light up in the most incredible way. She opened her eyes to find Rafferty staring at her.

"Wow," Rafferty said.

"I think I like it."

"So do I. I love you, Megan." Rafferty's face was suddenly full of seriousness.

"I love you too. I won't let you down. I promise."

Rafferty smiled. "I know you won't." She rolled Megan onto her back. "There's some places I've been longing to visit."

Megan laughed.

❧

It was Sunday evening and Helen unlocked the door to her daughter's condo. She had called at least twenty times. There had been no answer at home, on her pager or her cell phone. The deadbolt, Helen noticed, had not been set. Megan never just disappeared like this, Helen thought.

The blue screen of the television lit up the drawn curtain in the living room. An old Western was playing on the cable station. The sound was on mute and the set was extremely warm. Two wine glasses and a bowl of popcorn were on the coffee table. There were dirty dishes on the counter and a few beer bottles. Two of them were open but had not been drunk.

Megan was fastidiously neat. The condo never looked like this. Helen wondered who she was with and why she had left in such a hurry. Her car keys, wallet and cell phone were still on the table in the hallway. Helen sat down in the living room and tried to assess the situation. It appeared that Megan had been snatched from her home at a moment's notice. She had been missing at least twenty-four hours and no one appeared to know where she had gone. Helen had been trying to get ahold of her since Saturday morning to see if she wanted to go shopping at the Pottery Barn. Her neighbor, who worked there, had told her there was a big sale. Megan liked their stuff and so Helen thought she might like to go. She had tried her again in the evening and then again Sunday morning. From what she could tell Megan had left sometime Friday night and had yet to return. This was not like her. Helen dug out Megan's credit cards and called to find out about the most recent transactions. There were no plane tickets, no mystery hotel rooms or any rental car activity. Helen had learned all about tracing a person's activities from the private detective she had hired to tail her husband. Most people were not very sneaky. Having thought of all other possibilities for Megan's whereabouts, Helen called the police.

⊰⊱

Late Sunday evening, Rafferty took Megan home. When she pulled up in Megan's driveway Megan squeezed her hand and looked over at her with the fever of an entire weekend spent in bed dancing through her brain. Rafferty put her head on Megan's shoulder. "Tell me it was real."

"It was so real. That's why you're taking me home tonight or we'll never make it to work tomorrow."

"And you're still going to love and desire me tomorrow, correct?" Rafferty said. She nuzzled Megan's neck.

"You're being neurotic again," Megan counseled.

"That's because it seems too good to be true." Rafferty had that worried look on her face again.

Megan kissed her deeply. "Don't worry, everything is fine."

Suddenly, lights flashed behind them and a police officer on a bullhorn called out, "Get out of the car and put your hands on top of your head."

Rafferty looked in the rearview mirror. They were definitely addressing them. "Do you have an outstanding warrant or something? Because I think they're serious."

"I don't even have so much as a parking ticket. There must be some mistake." Megan turned around to look at the police car parked behind them.

They both got out of the car and put their hands up. A female police officer rushed up to Megan to identify her while her partner was pushing Rafferty on the hood of the car.

"What are you doing?" Megan asked, as the female officer escorted her toward the house. Helen came out the front door. "She didn't do anything."

"You know this woman?" the officer asked.

"Yes, she's my girlfriend."

"Where were you this weekend?"

"Is that really any of your business?" Megan asked, getting angry.

"It is because someone filed a missing persons report."

"Who did that?"

"I did," Helen replied.

"Why?" Megan was aghast.

"Because you literally fell off the planet for over two days. Your car is in the driveway and all your incidentals were on the hallway table. Including your wallet. What was I supposed to think?"

"I was with Rafferty."

"Why did you leave the house like that?" the police officer asked.

"Will you come inside so we can discuss this civilly?" Megan asked while she vied for time.

"Answer the question, please," he said.

"I can't believe this. I'm not fifteen anymore, missing my curfew."

"Look, either you tell us what happened or your friend goes downtown for questioning. People don't go missing like that. I want some satisfactory response here."

"All right. I kissed her after dinner and she freaked out. I went after her but I'd been drinking so I couldn't drive. She lives thirteen blocks away so I walked. I needed time to think. I didn't need my car keys. I wasn't driving or going shopping so I didn't need my wallet and the only person I wanted to talk to was Rafferty, so I didn't bring my phone. And then we spent the entire weekend making love. Happy now?"

Megan could tell Rafferty was mortified. She probably wished she was going downtown for questioning rather than standing here right now.

"Oh, I get it. She's straight," the police officer said, pointing at Megan.

"Correction, was straight," Megan replied. She turned to Helen. "I love her, Mom."

"Perhaps you two should go up to the house and have a little chat. We'll let your friend loose."

The cops rolled their eyes and one of them shrugged his shoulders. Rafferty said good-bye and then shot out of driveway like a bullet. Megan and Helen went inside. Megan's heart raced and she suddenly wished Rafferty had stayed.

Megan fixed them both a drink, then her mother turned to her. "What is this all about?"

"Before you say anything, I want you to know I love her."

Helen sat on the couch and patted the seat next to her. "Come talk to me."

Megan sat down next to her mother. She hadn't had time to plan a coming-out talk so she scrambled. She tried to think of something that would explain what had happened to her over the past months or so and now, spending the weekend in Rafferty's arms, she knew how her life would be.

"I just want you to be happy and to have someone to love. If that someone happens to be a woman then we'll just have a different kind of wedding one day."

"That's it? You're not freaked?" Megan said, taking a sip of her beer.

"No, darling. I counsel a lot of lesbians. I probably know more about them than you do right now. I think I understand why you've been so distant lately and now perhaps we can get back to how we were."

"I have been and I'm sorry, Mom. It must have been a protective device. I knew I was falling in love with Rafferty and I didn't know how you were going to take it so I cut myself off." Megan took her mother's hand.

"But I'm here now."

"I know, and if I need any advice on lesbians I'll know right where to go." She grinned.

"Good. Now perhaps we should call your friend. Ask her to come over. She's probably wondering what we're up to."

"I'm sure she is." Megan could only imagine the fit Rafferty was having. But it was only eight. She was sure an invitation to come over would calm Rafferty down. This was not exactly how she had planned introducing Rafferty to her mother.

Chapter Seven

On a Tuesday afternoon a few weeks later, Helen looked up from her appointment book to see Carmen standing in the open doorway. "There's a woman here to see you Her name is Bel Aragon."

Helen glanced down at her appointment book. Both she and Carmen had copies of the day's schedule. Helen wondered if there was some error in her copy. This was highly unlikely, because Carmen was an excellent secretary. She made appointments, did all the billing, took care of insurance claims and in general did everything except the counseling. Helen would have been lost without her, and to ensure Carmen stayed, Helen compensated her well.

Carmen said, "She doesn't have an appointment but she wants to talk to you. You don't have another one scheduled until four. She could take this hour if you want, or I could have her come back."

"No, that's okay. Show her in."

Carmen nodded and gestured for the woman to come in.

"Pleased to meet you," Helen said, extending her hand.

"The pleasure is mutual."

"Please take a seat." Helen surveyed the attractive woman sitting across from her. Her dark hair was short and stylish, her brown eyes were almost black in the soft light of her office. About fifty, she wore just enough makeup to enhance her features without being obvious. She was wearing a black tailored suit and expensive Italian shoes. It must be something truly traumatic for a woman like this to be resorting to therapy, Helen thought, maybe a cheating husband, a failing business or the death of a child. Helen didn't see women like Bel Aragon very often. It would be like Martha Stewart seeking her services.

"So what can I help you with today?" Dr. Kohlrabi asked. She got out her pen and yellow legal pad.

Bel started to laugh.

Helen was puzzled. This was not the usual response to this question. More often than not a torrent of tears was the normal reaction, followed by the story of what caused this pain.

"Actually, I came to check on you."

"Me? Why?"

"Sometimes it can be a shock, and I thought you might want to talk about it with someone who has some insight."

"Insight?"

"Insight into how it feels."

"How what feels?" Dr. Kohlrabi asked, now thoroughly confused as to what this woman wanted.

"I thought you knew," Bel said. "Perhaps I better go. I must have misunderstood the situation."

"Bel, have you ever been diagnosed by a doctor before?"

"I'm not crazy!"

"Then sit back down and tell me exactly what you are talking about because I obviously have no clue."

Bel sat down. "About Megan's being gay. I was concerned about how you were doing. I wished when I found out about Rafferty that I'd had someone to talk to."

It all clicked. "Oh, my goodness, I'm so sorry. I can't believe I didn't recognize your name. You're Megan's boss. How completely silly of me." She started to laugh. "It just didn't connect."

"And Rafferty's mother. You were in doctor mode. Don't worry, I do the same thing at work."

"First, I almost get your daughter arrested and then I try to psychoanalyze her mother. Boy, I couldn't botch this up any worse."

"I should have presented myself more correctly. So how are you taking it?"

"I don't know exactly. I want her to be happy and a few weeks ago I was planning a wedding. On the other hand, I've never seen her so happy and vivacious and interested in things other than the law."

Bel laughed. "That's a good thing. If it's any consolation you'll never get over not having a wedding and grandchildren."

"I try not to go there."

"It's hard not to sometimes and I'm not necessarily a fan of marriage myself."

Suddenly the door flew open. God came barging in the office with Carmen screaming behind her, "You can't go in there!"

"The hell I can't!" God screamed back.

"What is it?" Helen said, annoyed at God's inappropriate behavior.

"They're trying to remove me from the lexicon. I told you my identity crisis is real."

"Slow down. What are you talking about?" She looked at Bel. "Excuse me for a moment."

"This atheist is trying to have the words *under God* removed from the Pledge of Allegiance. He's taking it to court."

Bel stood up. "I should go."

"Maybe we could talk again," Dr. Kohlrabi said, handing Bel her card.

Bel exited quickly and Helen suddenly wished she wouldn't go. God touched her shoulder and, puzzled, Helen turned to look at her.

"Don't worry. You two will become good friends," God said. She flopped down on the couch. "Being angry makes me tired. I'm sorry I burst in like that."

There was a loud crash across the street.

"Oh, no," God said, groaning.

Helen jumped up and went to the window. Bel was down the sidewalk just past the San Felipe Church where the giant stained-glass window above the Spanish front doors had come crashing down. Cars were stopped in the street. Two people from inside the church came running out to survey the huge pile of colored glass.

"I don't believe it!" Helen was shocked. How had this happened? It was such a beautiful window. Bel could have been killed or at least maimed for life.

"You need to call your new friend right now."

"Why?" Helen was baffled. She didn't have Bel's number but she could call Megan's office and ask to be transferred.

"She needs to stay away from anything religious for the rest of the day until it wears off," God said ominously.

"Until what wears off?"

"You know how things grow, like the near-dead plants in your office, after you've been with me." God gestured to the spider plant that had once been on its last legs and was now threatening to take over the office. Carmen trimmed it every day.

"Yes."

"Well, there's a reverse."

It took a moment for Helen to realize what God meant. "Oh my."

"Exactly."

"But how am I going to call Bel, whom I just met, and tell her that she was responsible for wrecking a church window because she was sitting here when you came in mad? Do you realize how ludicrous that sounds?" Helen was starting to get angry. It didn't seem fair.

"I suppose it does. I guess we'll just have to hope she stays at the office the rest of day and away from churches. Now about my identity crisis . . ."

Megan and Rafferty were returning from a late lunch when they met Bel in the lobby of the office building of the law firm.

"How was lunch?" Bel asked.

"Lovely, we've been going to Chez Nous lately. Megan's mother took her there a few weeks ago so we've been popping in there ever since for lunch," Rafferty said.

Megan noticed one of the ficus trees in the lobby was shriveling up before her eyes like some fast-forward movie they'd seen in grade school showing how plants grew. Only this was in reverse. The fern went next.

"I met your mother today," Bel said.

"You did?" Megan said, surprised.

"I went to see her, to see how she was handling your conversion."

"That was a little forward of you, don't you think?" Rafferty said, her face getting flushed. Megan gave her the don't-fight-with-your-mother look.

Megan looked over Rafferty's shoulder to see the giant hanging baskets of petunias that hung in the atrium dry up. The leaves shriveled and all the flowers turned brown. Other people were starting to notice the phenomenon, all except Rafferty and Bel.

"I wanted to give her comfort. No one comforted me when I found out you liked girls instead of boys. Believe it or not, Rafferty, it's a shock. I was just trying to help. Helen was fine with it. We had a mother-to-mother chat. I would appreciate it if you would just get over it."

The elevator came and they stepped in. Rafferty was scowling but didn't say anything.

"I hope that's all right with you, Megan."

"It's fine, Bel. In fact, it was kind of you."

Rafferty tsked to indicate her displeasure with the sappy conversation.

"Rafferty, stop that. It's rude," Bel said.

The elevator stopped and they got out. Bel went to check her messages and every plant in the reception area of the office shriveled up and died as she walked by. Even Rafferty noticed. "What the hell?"

"I don't know, but I think it has something to do with Bel," Megan said.

"I always knew she was plant killer. Why do you think she has a gardener? Oh, this is good," Rafferty said. "Watch this."

"What?"

"Eileen's lucky bamboo plant. You know, the one she bought at the flea market. She's been nursing it all winter. It's supposed to bring good luck and romance."

Eileen shrieked as her beloved plant turned from bright green to brown and its stalk bent over forming a perfect letter *n*. "My bamboo plant! It's dying."

Sam, the janitor, came rushing down the hall. "It's all right, Eileen. Here, give it to me and I'll put it in the mop sink with a lot of water. I'm sure we can get it back."

Bel was oblivious to the whole thing. She looked at her messages. "Don't they sell those things all over town? Get a new one."

"Mom, look around you. Like, every plant you walk by instantly dies. You're like a walking herbicide," Rafferty said.

"I don't know what you're talking about. It's probably some strange fungus that all the plants are catching. Now if you don't mind, I have work to do." Bel swept past the giant cactus that was growing in the waiting area and it dropped to the ground. "Sam, will you call the plant company and tell them we've got an epidemic here."

"Right away," Sam said as he handed Eileen a tissue. "I'll get you a new bamboo plant. My cousin works at this Oriental import place. They get them all the time. Good ones."

Eileen nodded tearfully.

Rafferty snickered. Megan poked her in the ribs. When the plant company came there was a huge ruckus over what had happened to the plants. The plant person was certain that the plants had been poisoned by a disgruntled employee and Bel was financially responsible for the damages. She thought not. They refused to replace them so Bel had Sam haul them out to the dumpster, claiming she could give a rat's ass about the plants anyway.

Two days later Helen received a call from Bel Aragon and now they were walking down Central Avenue together going to a restaurant for dinner. Bel had indicated she wanted to try Chez Nous since the girls had been raving about it.

"I'm so glad you called," Helen said. She studiously avoided looking at the San Felipe Church where they were repairing the stained-glass window. She had seen on the evening news that they thought perhaps a sudden change in temperature had caused the giant window to pull away from its casing and thus send it crashing to the ground. This morning she had donated money to the collection box they had placed near the front door. Apparently, the church's insurance company didn't pay for damages caused by acts of God. Helen couldn't help but chuckle at this, but still she felt obligated to help.

She hoped that Bel didn't noticed the spontaneous blooming of plants as they passed by. She'd just spent a session with you-know-who and now she was positively brimming with good vibes. Bel was polite and hadn't inquired into the strange phenomenon until, as they waited to cross the street a nearby hibiscus bush burst into bloom, instantly producing beautiful red flowers. It was way too early for flowers.

"You're not . . ." Bel asked.

"No, I'm just the therapist."

Bel nodded. "So all this is by-product?"

"That's a good way to put it," Helen said. They crossed the street, leaving the hibiscus bush behind.

"We had better never go to the botanical gardens. It would really freak out the staff. You know, the other day, I killed every plant in the office. So was that like a reverse process?"

Helen laughed. "Kind of. Because she was angry."

"The plant company is threatening to sue."

"Oh, my goodness." That has to be a first, Helen thought.

"They don't have a leg to stand on. Rafferty called me a walking herbicide."

Helen laughed.

"Are you devout?" Bel said, meeting Helen's gaze.

"No, I am, or rather I was, an agnostic Jew."

"No doubts now."

"No. How about you?" Helen asked as they continued their stroll down the wide boulevard. Hardly anyone in Phoenix walked anywhere so the streets around downtown were always pleasantly uncrowded.

"I'm a lost Catholic."

Helen chuckled. "Worse than just lapsed, I suppose. Yes, well I can certainly understand feeling lost, given what's happened lately."

"It's terrible, but it started long before that. I've been concerned over heaven and hell, the idea of a life lived solely in hopes of a greater reward. Is there such a place?"

"That was my first question. According to you-know-who, those are human constructs and the human mind is not able to grasp the afterlife, so stories will have to do."

"Like trying to explain calculus to a three-year-old."

"Exactly."

"Why does everything have to be an endless parable?" Bel said rhetorically.

"I was thinking of it this way. How I perceive and order the world in my mind is entirely different from how you do it. We have common symbols that allow us to communicate, but we will never think exactly the same way. If we multiply this difference by a number we don't have, you get the mind of God."

"You're extremely good at explaining things."

"I'm the therapist. I have to explain people to themselves."

"Does that mean you can explain yourself to yourself?" Bel said.

Helen laughed. "If only it were that easy." They had passed by the museum. "Oh, look, they're having a display of Monet's Giverny paintings. I love that part of his work. If I had a ton of money I'd buy one of his water lily paintings and then decorate my living room around it."

"Have you been to the Giverny gardens?"

"With *my* ex-husband?" Helen said incredulously, thinking the only place you could get Lars to was a golf course.

"Oh, well, they are lovely. Perhaps we should go to the exhibit," Bel offered.

"I'd like that."

"It's a date then."

It was late Thursday afternoon and Gigi met Mallory at the gym after work to play racquetball. Mallory sat on the locker room bench reading the first few chapters of Gigi's new book. Gigi paced back and forth, waiting for her to finish so she could get a response. It had been several weeks since she started it. She'd written for two hours a night every night.

"It's really hard to concentrate when you do that," Mallory said, looking up from the manuscript.

"Do what?"

"Pace like that. Sit down and try to be still. Besides, I thought the whole reason we can't play racquetball is because your feet hurt. What's wrong with them anyway?"

"They don't hurt. They just bleed all the time and I have to keep them bandaged up and I can't fit them in shoes. Caroline knitted me these," Gigi said, pointing out her multicolored slippers. Caroline had given up on the poultices and kept trying to get her to go to the doctor. Gigi couldn't afford a doctor, so Caroline whipped her up a pair of slippers.

"How sweet," Mallory said, going back to the manuscript.

You're a moron, Gigi told herself, *with an overactive sex drive.* Mallory may have forgiven Gigi, but clearly she still harbored severe misgivings toward Caroline. Caroline had masterminded the whole affair; she knew how deeply Mallory had loved her and still Caroline fucked around on her. Caroline should never have chosen Gigi, especially now that she was regaining Mallory's trust. It was downright cruel. Gigi could see that now.

Mallory finished reading the second chapter. "This is really good and completely beyond your ken. Are you sure you didn't pirate this off the Internet?"

"No, I wrote it," Gigi said defiantly.

"Just checking," Mallory replied. Gigi unwrapped one of the bandages on her feet. She could feel the gauze getting all bunched up. Mallory peered down at the perfectly round patch of cracked and bleeding skin on the arch of Gigi's foot. "Have you had a doctor look at your feet?"

"Are you high?"

"No. I mean, certainly a dermatologist would know why they're doing that."

"I can't," Gigi said.

"Why not?"

"I don't want to. It's just this thing that's going on and one day it'll go away. Look, I've tried everything. It'll go away as soon as I'm done with the book."

"That's probably what's causing them."

"What do mean?"

"Stress. You're stressed out from writing the book and it's manifesting itself in this weird skin condition."

"You know, you're probably right." Gigi wrapped her foot back up and put her slipper on. "Let's go get a beer somewhere. It's hotter than shit out there and if I can't do good things to my body, I'd like to abuse it a bit."

"Sure. How about the George and Dragon Pub."

"Oh, I love that place. I'm going to have a pint of Newcastle." Gigi remembered that Caroline had night class on Thursday. "Or maybe two."

"I'm really proud of you, Gigi."

Gigi gave her an inquiring look. "Why?"

"For changing your life around."

"Maybe we should hold the praise until I've been guilt-free for at least a year. I'm certain I'm still capable of doing horrible things."

"Yeah, but at least now you appear to have a conscience," Mallory said, handing her the manuscript.

"It kind of sucks." Gigi stuck the manuscript in her backpack.

Mallory laughed. "Come on, let's go. I'll buy."

Across town Helen was talking to God about her anger-management problem. God usually had her appointments in the morning but Helen had a dentist appointment so all her appointments were running later. God had taken the last slot of the day.

"It just infuriates me how such basic tenets as 'love thy neighbor' can get so screwed up. I mean, how did religion get so secular and hateful. It's not right," God said.

"I think it may be a case of the telephone game," Helen said, propping her head in her hand. Sometimes being in the presence of God made her extremely tired.

"The telephone game? What's that?"

"It's a game kids play at parties. One person starts a story and then passes it on. It ripples through the whole group and the last person in line tells the story again. It never even remotely resembles the original and everybody has a good laugh."

God looked at her oddly.

"It was just a metaphor for how things get distorted." Helen felt wetness on her cheek. She looked down at her hand. The nickel-sized red mark in the center of her palm had begun to bleed. The palms of her hands had been getting worse. She tried heavy-duty hand lotions, and the pharmacist had recommended Zim's crack cream but it didn't appear to be working. She had a sneaking suspicion that hanging out with God was producing her symptoms.

God looked away. "What is it?" Helen asked.

"I get kind of queasy at the sight of blood. Your hands will get better when I go away."

"I see." Helen studied her palms again.

"We should wrap them up. Do you have a First Aid kit?"

"I do now, in the bathroom."

God attempted to wrap Helen's hands with gauze. She wasn't doing a very good job.

"You make a terrible nurse." Helen was glad the sores didn't hurt.

"And you look like a mummy."

"Here, let me try." Helen took the gauze and attempted to wrap her hands.

"You're not any better."

They both started to laugh.

"Helen?" a voice said from the inner office. Carmen had left for the day early as she had a wedding to go to. Helen guessed it was Bel.

"Who's that?" God said in a panic.

"It's Bel. We're supposed to be going to dinner."

"This is really bad timing," God said, looking at the blood in the sink. The sink was covered in blood and Helen's attempts at bandaging her own hands had proved futile. All she had succeeded

105

in doing was covering the vanity with blood and ruining her white silk shirt.

"Helen, are you all right?" Bel called out.

"I'm in here, Bel," Helen said, knowing what Bel was about to see was not going to be pretty.

Bel came in the bathroom. "What happened?"

"It's nothing really," Helen said lamely. "It's just this skin condition I've got."

"But your hands," Bel said.

"Yes, well, perhaps you could assist me."

"Yes, that's a great idea. I'm thinking I should go," God said.

"Yes, that's a good idea."

"I'll see you in a couple of days. Let those heal a bit," God said. She looked over at Bel. "Sorry about that window thing and killing all the plants. Helen is helping me learn to deal with my anger issues."

"That's all right," Bel said. God left and Bel wrapped Helen's hands. "What was she talking about,' the window thing'?"

"It's nothing," Helen said, avoiding Bel's gaze.

"I thought you said you weren't—"

"I'm not. This is a by-product of being in her presence. It'll go away when she stops coming for therapy."

"Well, right now it's bleeding like a sieve," Bel replied. She wrapped another layer of gauze over her hands.

"I know."

"Do you have another shirt? We might be able to save this one if we get it soaking right away. Not to mention you look like you committed some heinous crime."

Helen laughed. "I suppose I do. Yes, I have some extra clothes in that closet over there."

Bel found a gray pullover. "Will this work?"

"Yes, at least it doesn't have any buttons. I might need some help getting this off."

"Here, let me help," Bel said. She undid the buttons and then slid the shirt off Helen's shoulders.

Helen noticed Bel's high coloring. "I didn't mean to embarrass you."

"No, it's not that. I'm not used to being so close to someone," Bel replied. She draped the gray pullover over Helen's head gently and for a moment their eyes locked.

"It's all right, Bel."

"I know. Now let's see if we can save your shirt," Bel said. She immersed the white silk shirt in cold water. Helen sat on the commode and watched, feeling useless.

"Perhaps instead of going out for dinner we could go to my house. I froze some of the trout the girls caught, and I make a mean blackened trout."

"That sounds nice."

"I have an idea of how to make an adaptive fork for you to use."

"Bel, you're a good friend. Thank you."

Bel smiled.

Chapter Eight

It was Wednesday night and Gigi knew her mother played bingo. Her father had invited her over for hamburgers. Gigi was leery about showing up at the house but she missed her father. He told her that Rose was keeping strict tabs on him because she'd found out about them going out for dinner together. She leaned her bike up against the house. Her mother's gold Buick LeSabre was gone so it appeared the coast was clear. She noticed her mother hadn't repaired the bathtub shrine of the Virgin Mary since Aunt Lil and Gigi had clandestinely destroyed it.

Gigi's parents lived in a modest brick home off Thomas Street. The old palm trees in the front yard were horribly overgrown and filled with families of pigeons. The front yard was graveled over and in places the black plastic that was supposed to serve as a weed barrier was pulled up and knee-high weeds had taken root. The garage door still tilted to one side and wouldn't shut properly after

Rose ran into it one day. She was screaming at Gigi and put the car in drive instead of reverse. She slammed into the metal garage door and wrecked it permanently. That was three years ago.

It occurred to Gigi that her parents' house was a museum of sorts for all the bad things that happened in their family, and for a moment she felt kind of sad. It must have been her conscience kicking in again. She limped into the living room. Riding her bike was painful in slippers. She had taped pieces of cardboard to the pedals in an attempt to remedy the situation. It wasn't working that well. Her father was nowhere to be found. Gigi went to the kitchen. Her mother was standing at the kitchen counter making hamburger patties. She shrieked when she saw Gigi.

"What are you doing here?" Gigi said in a panic.

"I live here."

"But you're supposed to be at bingo," Gigi said, backing out of the kitchen.

Rose stared at her.

Paulie came in the kitchen. "Gigi, you're early."

"Dad, you said she'd be gone."

"Now, don't get your grundies in a bundle," Paulie said, putting his arm around Gigi's shoulders. "I had to tell a little lie to get you here. Now, Rose, before you go off half-cocked, Gigi is our only child and damn it I want us to be a family again." He hitched up his pants and licked his lower lip. These were signals he meant business.

Rose was still quiet. She was just standing there peering at Gigi.

Paulie continued, "Now, Gigi's willing to become a Baptist."

"Dad!" Gigi screeched.

"Gigi, work with me. Now, the Lehoneys down the street are Baptists and they seem like real nice folks. It seems there's a lot less equipment and fanfare when you're a Baptist and I'm willing to give this a try."

Rose didn't appear to be paying attention to a word he'd said. "Gigi, have you found God?" she asked in amazement.

Gigi panicked. She'd spent the better part of the afternoon with God. She'd been taking some extra time off from the photo studio so she could work on the book. God, it seemed, was in a hurry to get it done. God had warned her not to go around her mother because she glowed or something. This was not good. "I . . . I think God found me."

"The shrines! That's why you destroyed them. They are graven images and the Almighty doesn't like them. The golden calf. I can't believe I didn't make the connection. Come here, Gigi." Rose held out her arms.

Gigi stood perfectly still. She could count on one hand the number of times her mother had hugged her. Paulie gave her a shove. As Gigi's face was buried in her mother's breasts, she asked, "Do we have to become Baptists?"

Rose and Paulie laughed. "No, that was just another little lie. Now, how about those hamburgers. All this talk about God has made me hungry," Paulie said. He picked up the plate of hamburgers and headed out to the backyard.

Gigi knew he'd gotten a little misty and didn't want to appear unmanly. Her father was old-school.

Rose looked at Gigi's feet. "Why are you wearing slippers?"

"It's the latest fashion craze," Gigi lied. "Haven't you seen all the kids wearing pajama bottoms and slippers to school?"

"I suppose I have." Rose pulled the potato salad out of the fridge.

"I missed your potato salad."

"Gigi, we've got to try harder."

"All right."

Rose started to laugh. "You know, that's the first thing we've agreed on in years."

"I think it's the first thing ever."

Paulie came back in the kitchen blowing his nose on the big white hankie he kept in his back pocket. He gave Gigi a bear hug. "I'm glad you're back, kid."

"Me too."

The next day Gigi shuffled into her appointment with Dr. Kohlrabi in the slippers that Caroline had knitted. They were multicolored and clashed badly with Gigi's sober attire. She looked at Dr. Kohlrabi's hands. "What, we both get half?" she said snidely.

Dr. Kohlrabi nodded. "It appears so."

"I'm not finding this amusing in the least."

"You don't? I find this to be an amazing exchange, a once-in-a-lifetime experience."

Gigi sighed. "No, it's a pain in the ass. I used to be a heathen and a completely amoral pagan. It's kind of hard to retain those identities when the finger of God has been poking around in your life. Not to mention that I've reconciled my differences with my mother, who thinks I've become an angel or something. Now I can do no wrong whereas before, I was born wrong. Is that disgusting or what?"

Dr. Kohlrabi smiled benevolently. "No, I think it's wonderful."

"Now she thinks I was smashing the religious bathtub shrines because God was pissed off about the graven images. She's going to start her own shrine-smashing group and she wants me to head it up. I told her I was past that. I mean, the world is turning fucking upside down," Gigi ranted.

Dr. Kohlrabi nodded.

"Aren't you concerned about all of this?" Gigi said. She adjusted her slippers. The sizing was a bit off.

"Not really."

"Why not?" Gigi asked, getting panicky.

"Because when one is dealing with the most powerful entity in the universe it's complete folly to think that you might change the course of action."

"Go with the flow, in other words."

"Yes, you should enjoy this time with her. It won't last forever, and you'll miss her when she's gone."

"I thought she was, like, omni-accessible."

"She is, but you don't usually get a callback."

"That's true."

At the end of the day, Helen stood waiting for the elevator. Her office was on the fourth floor of a small stucco building that housed a podiatrist, a massage therapist Helen kept meaning to go see, and some miscellaneous small businesses that kept coming and going. The door opened and God was standing inside dressed in a formal black tuxedo.

"Going down?" God stepped to one side.

"Yes, thank you. Where are you going all dressed up so fine?" Helen asked.

"I'm going to the Gala Lesbian Dress Ball." God straightened her gold cummerbund. "It's a benefit."

"You're really getting into this gay thing."

"Yes, well, I've decided I've paid far too little attention to this particular sect of my creation. I'm finding them most interesting," God said as she watched the elevator numbers light up as they descended.

"You're picking up human habits," Helen noted.

"I am, but they rub off easily enough." God ran her hand along the wood railing in the elevator. She appeared to be preoccupied. This was unusual for her.

"What do you do after these forays into your science project, take a cosmic bath?"

"Precisely. I go the God Spa and wash all my earthly cares away."

They both laughed.

"But really, I came to tell you something." God met her gaze.

"Yes?" Helen inquired. She felt her heart rate speed up a notch. God's ulterior motives kept popping up in her life and in Gigi's. It appeared God did not like to make her plans apparent in one sitting but rather revealed them slowly and in pieces.

"That night with your hands, when Bel fixed you up . . ."

"Yes?" Helen replied, wondering where this was going.

"She liked it too."

"Liked what?" Helen asked, now knowing full well where this was going.

"Being so close to you."

"I thought you'd left." It suddenly occurred to Helen that having God in her life was more complicated than was first apparent. How many other things had God been privy to?

"I'm omniscient, remember?"

"You were spying."

"That's beside the point. I know what you were thinking. You liked how soft her hands felt on your shoulders. Your heart started racing and you felt flushed."

"Since when have you been interested in my vital signs?"

"Tell the truth," God prodded.

"All right. It was like being touched for the first time and I liked it." Helen played back the scene in her head. It was a curious feeling being so close to Bel and she had never experienced that with another woman. She was a woman and so was Bel. There had been nothing more to it. "You didn't manufacture those feelings, did you?"

"No, I had nothing to do with that, but you should send her orchids, white ones."

"Why?" Helen was confused. She knew she was attracted to Bel but what to do about it was an entirely different issue.

"Because she likes them, silly. And she's just as confused as you are."

"All right. I'll send the flowers."

The elevator door opened and they stepped out.

"Have fun tonight," Helen said.

"Oh, I intend to," God said, smiling broadly. "Don't worry about the thing with Bel. Everything will work out the way it's supposed to."

It was Friday and Gigi had worked all morning at the photography studio taking aura pictures of a group of New Age people who had heard about Danielle's studio. Gigi took fourteen portraits of long-haired people in Birkenstock sandals and smelling of patchouli. Her sinuses were inflamed and she was kind of crabby. Danielle gave her the rest of the afternoon off. Gigi called Caroline and told her she was coming home early. Caroline had been doing yard work all morning—she now had Fridays off from school—but said she'd take a shower so they could spend the afternoon doing you-know-what. This had improved Gigi's mood immensely.

When she got home Gigi stood in the doorway of the bathroom. She hadn't been able to find Caroline anywhere else in the house. "Oh, my God!"

"Yes?" God said from behind the door.

"What have you done to her?" Gigi demanded. She pointed to the huge set of bone white feathery wings coming out of Caroline's shoulder blades.

"I made her an angel."

"What for?"

"Because she wanted to know what angels looked like, although this isn't really what they look like, rather it's what Caroline thinks they look like."

Caroline was looking in the mirror, obviously admiring her new appendages.

"And why is she naked?" Gigi's face was hot.

"I wouldn't give her the towel until she believed in me. I can't have you living in the house with a nonbeliever. She was a tough sell. I had to do the burning bush trick and John the Baptist's head on a platter. That's what finally got her."

"Why are you wet?" Gigi said, pointing at God.

"I tried to put her out with the shower head when she was doing the burning bush thing," Caroline said.

Gigi snatched the towel from God and handed it to Caroline. "Make those go away now before you get us all crucified," Gigi snapped at God.

"You're no fun," God said, pouting.

"You're dangerous. No wonder the world is so fucked up," Gigi said.

"Gigi, that's not nice," Caroline said. Wingless, she slipped on a T-shirt and a pair of shorts. "It's not her fault that we're so screwed up. She made us perfect. We're solely responsible for our own imperfections."

"Thank you," God said.

"Whatever," Gigi replied.

"And now you and I have a little errand to run," God said to her.

"What now?" Gigi asked, perturbed.

"Did you run a hard copy of the manuscript like I asked?"

"Of course," Gigi said. "It's in my backpack."

"Good. Now let's go sell the thing."

"I'm not sure I'm ready for this," Gigi said.

"Stop being such a coward. I've already paved the way for you," God said.

"Oh, gee, I can only imagine," Gigi said, pulling the manuscript out of her backpack, which was still sitting on the bathroom floor where she had dropped it during the angel episode.

"Trust me," God said. She picked up the manuscript and leafed through the pages.

"It is a good book," Caroline said, brushing her hair.

"I want to make a difference in people's lives," God said.

Gigi laughed.

"What's so funny?" God said, her eyebrows knit in consternation.

"You already botched that one," Gigi replied.

"This book is different; self-help is not the Bible. Besides, I didn't have a lot to do with that, not the aftermath at least."

115

"She's right. I think keeping your book out of the theology section and in the New Age self-improvement section of the bookstore will help immensely. It'll be more successful and less dangerous. I've been reading the book as Gigi's been writing it. I hope you don't mind," Caroline said.

"I know you have. No, it's fine," God said.

"Let's hope so for my sake, because I'm the one who's going to get my ass nailed to the wall if this thing goes wrong." Gigi picked up a lone white feather that had fallen from the angel wings. She examined it closely and then gave it to Caroline. "Look, it's a souvenir."

"Thanks. I still think you need a better attitude about this. The book is something to help people better understand themselves and get motivated to become better people. Don't you care about people?"

"No. I don't really like people. I mean, I like you," Gigi added, noticing the hurt look on Caroline's face.

"Well, you better learn to like people because they're going to come to you for guidance," God advised.

"Look, I just typed the fucking thing."

"Actually, you did more than that."

"What are you talking about?" Gigi said, getting flustered. She knew God had something more up her sleeve than just typing a manuscript.

God shrugged. "My mind doesn't work like a human's. I needed your brain to put the ideas into human terms. I planted things, you made them grow."

"I just did what you told me," Gigi said, getting panicky.

"Gigi, relax. She won't let anything happen to you. You're one of the chosen ones. They don't get hurt . . . well, except for your skin condition and oh—the crucifixion." Caroline stared intently at God.

"That wasn't supposed to happen," God replied evenly.

"See, now you know why I'm scared," Gigi said. She walked out of the bathroom and went to sit on the couch. They followed her. Gigi rested her head in her hands.

"I have a better exit strategy this time," God said, sitting down next to her.

"I certainly hope so. If I get blown to pieces by some religious nut job I'm going to be really pissed at you." After all, she thought, it would be her name on the book jacket, not God's.

"I'll take care of you," God said, putting her arm around Gigi's shoulders.

"That's what I'm afraid of," Gigi said. Both Caroline and Gigi eyed God suspiciously.

"Just relax, both of you. Now grab the book and let's go."

"Where are we going?" Gigi asked.

"To get published," God said.

"Oh, just like that, huh," Gigi chided. "On a Friday afternoon. Right."

"I think you're forgetting who I am."

Gigi and God stood outside the front door of the Dial Tower in downtown Phoenix looking up. The Golden Calf Publishing Company was located on the seventeenth floor. Gigi was dubious. "You really think this is going to work?"

"It'll work."

"I just don't want you to be disappointed. Don't we have to write letters or something? I mean, popping up with the manuscript seems a little forward." Not to mention she was wearing slippers.

"I don't have time to be piddling around waiting until someone, somewhere thinks they might be a little bit interested," God said.

"All right, all right. Don't get your grundies in a bundle," Gigi said, following God inside the building. The lobby was immense and God's shoes made sucking noises as they crossed the granite floor to the elevator which opened immediately upon their arrival.

117

"What does that mean?" God asked, pushing the button.

"That your underwear gets all bunched up and you get all fussy."

"Oh, now, come closer," God said, holding out her arms.

"What for?" Gigi asked nervously.

"Because I said so."

Gigi stepped closer. God wrapped her arms around her. Gigi felt like every neuron in her body was lit up and overloaded. "What did you do?"

"I jump-started you. These are reverent people. They'll sense it."

"What? You made me glow." Gigi looked at her arm. It did seem to have a kind of aura.

"Kind of. You have that touched-by-God look."

"Oh, goody. Will it help our case?"

"Yes. Now, do you remember these people?"

"What people?"

"The people we're going to see about publishing the book. They're the Eichenbachers and they own this publishing company. He was the man I had you touch at the hospital that day when he had a heart attack."

"Oh, I get it. My, how neatly you've connected things," Gigi said snidely.

"I'm not leaving this to chance." God pushed open the door and they went inside.

Gigi introduced herself at the desk and explained her plight.

The well-dressed brunette receptionist informed Gigi and her now invisible companion that the publishing house did not accept unsolicited manuscripts.

"This one they will," Gigi replied.

"No, I'm afraid not."

"I don't think your glow thing is working," Gigi whispered to God.

She's not spiritual. Just tell her this. God went on with a sort of sales pitch.

Gigi relayed the message. "God says that if you don't tell the Eichenbachers we're here she'll give you a wicked case of acne. By the way, tonight you're going to meet Mr. Right, who will marry you and give you the children you so desire. He'll make a great husband and father. You don't want to mess it up by showing up looking like a pimple pizza. Tonight is the beginning of your new life, so don't screw it up. Go in there and tell Randolph that God plucked him from the jaws of death for a reason, and that reason is now here. Don't keep us waiting."

The now stunned receptionist disappeared behind a closed set of executive doors with a brass plate that said *Eichenbacher*.

The Eichenbachers were much different from the receptionist, Gigi noted. It appeared they could see the glow. Gigi relaxed a little. Randolph asked her to have a seat then took the manuscript gently from her, as if it were an infant. He was a dark-haired man with a well-trimmed beard. About six foot four, he was wearing a pair of tanned Dockers and an azure shirt. He put on his reading glasses over which he looked at his wife.

"It's a self-help manual with a message," Gigi explained.

"Is it really the . . ." He paused, looking a little choked up.

"The word of God?" Gigi finished. "Well, I suppose it is. She says she filtered it through a human mind because she doesn't think like we do."

"You said 'she,'" Laura Eichenbacher said excitedly. She was a small, pretty blonde wearing a flowered sundress.

"Well, she is she to me because I like women. She would incarnate as anyone wished."

"Are you devout?" Laura asked quietly.

"Me? Hell, no," Gigi said. "Ouch." God had poked her in the ribs. "No, I'm going to tell them what a whimsical and capricious God you are."

Wow, big words coming from you, God chided.

"My vocabulary has improved from hanging out with you. Besides you made me study all those books."

Great. And now you throw them back at me.

"You shouldn't have given us free will. It's like handing the keys to the Cadillac to a teenager and then getting pissed when they crash it."

That may have been a mistake. God nodded. *But you would have become boring creatures without it.*

Gigi turned to see the Eichenbachers staring intently at her. "I suppose this looks rather odd. As I was saying, God has chosen a pagan, amoral, heathen lesbian as her messenger."

They both sat with shocked expressions on their faces.

"Sorry to disappoint you, but my behavior has improved in her presence," Gigi offered.

"Saint Paul started out badly," Randolph said, leafing through the manuscript.

"And what about Mary Magdelene." Laura leaned over her husband's shoulder to read the manuscript.

"Faith is an amazing thing," Gigi said. She could tell the Eichenbachers were anxious to read the manuscript and she was getting kind of antsy. She wondered if Caroline was still in the mood for a little afternoon hanky-panky.

Now about the book. God nudged Gigi.

"So will you publish the manuscript?" Gigi asked.

"Most certainly. Did God pick us for a reason?" Randolph asked.

"She told me to tell you she picked you because you're devout and you feel God every day," Gigi said, relaying the message.

"Outstanding," Randolph said, clapping his hands together. "Let's get started." He rang the receptionist. "June, please bring in a contract and the checkbook. Now, the negotiations usually take a month or so to go into effect. You are free to get a lawyer to look over the contract."

120

"Oh, I don't think you'd screw God," Gigi said.

"Well, of course not. I mean, the royalties are fairly standard within the industry and everything depends on sales, but I think this book will do very well," Randolph said.

"Great then, well, I've got to get going," Gigi said. "Is everything kosher with you?"

I find it most acceptable. God smiled broadly. *And yes, Caroline is still in the mood.*

Chapter Nine

Megan lay in Rafferty's arms still glowing from their afternoon dalliance. It was Saturday and they were supposed to be doing some research at the law library. Megan smiled to herself. Being interested in something other than work was still a new sensation to her.

"Does this part go away?" she asked.

"What part?"

"You know . . ." She ran her finger around Rafferty's soft brown nipple. It became hard beneath her touch.

"Oh, that part," Rafferty said.

"All I think about is how long it will be before I can hold you naked in my arms again." Megan trailed her hand down Rafferty's stomach.

Rafferty parted her legs and pulled Megan on top of her. "What are you thinking about now?"

"About getting inside you again," Megan said, putting her fingers inside Rafferty. Rafferty pulled her in tight, wrapping her thighs around her. Within minutes Megan brought her to climax.

"Oh, my God, that feels good," Rafferty said.

Smiling, Megan sat on top of her. "I love you, Rafferty."

"Ditto."

"Do you think our mothers are spending a lot of time together lately?"

Rafferty ran her hands across Megan's backside and positioned her so their crotches met. "I don't really want to talk about my mother right now." She gently moved against Megan.

"Just check it out."

"All I want to do is check you out," Rafferty said, putting her fingers inside Megan and watching her intently. Megan ground her hips slowly against Rafferty's hand until she felt herself coming again.

After dinner on the way to Symphony Hall, Helen leaned back in the leather seat of Bel's Lexus and thought about how much she enjoyed spending time with Bel. She hoped Bel felt the same way and had a sneaking suspicion that she did. Maybe God was right in letting things follow their course and not worrying about it. This was still a difficult concept for Helen to get her mind around. She was good at helping other people combat their neurosis. It was harder when it came to one's own psyche. At least her palms were clearing up. Now she only needed small Band-Aids on them.

Helen was mildly amused when Bel looked over at her and said, "Rafferty thinks it's weird that we spend so much time together."

"I'm surprised those two have had time to think of anything."

"What do you mean? I've kept their caseload lighter than usual. I thought it would be nice for them to get off on the right foot. I don't want Rafferty to screw this one up."

"Busy with each other. I swear, every time I talk to Megan she's in bed and I don't think she's alone."

"How do you know that?"

"Megan doesn't answer her cell phone but she'll pick up on the first ring on the land line. The only phone in her condo is in the bedroom."

Bel laughed. "I bet that hasn't crossed her mind."

"I'm sure it hasn't."

Bel pulled into the parking lot of Symphony Hall and parked the car. She looked over at Helen. "Are you sure you're all right with this thing?"

"Megan and Rafferty?"

Bel nodded. "Yes."

"I've never seen Megan so happy and interested in things other than the law."

"They appear to be doing well," Bel agreed. "Rafferty is actually behaving like a decent human being."

Helen laughed. "You know, we're lucky. They grew up and became motivated, caring young women."

"Yes," Bel said, obviously distracted.

"What are you thinking?" Helen asked as they walked toward the concert hall, swarming with concert-goers. She glanced up the stairs of the massive granite monolith. She had always thought it looked like a big box in odd contrast to something as fluid as music.

"Just how Megan was straight one day and then gay the next. It seems so odd."

"I suppose that's true. I think she found herself falling in love with a person who happened to be a woman. Fortunately, she didn't see that as an obstacle to love, which is a good thing. It takes courage to do that," Helen said.

"You put things into perspective beautifully. It's a pity the world doesn't see it that way."

"Exactly," Helen said, sliding her arm through Bel's as they entered the building and were ushered to their seats in the balcony for an evening of Bach performed by the Chicago Symphony Orchestra. Helen was excited. She loved classical music. She looked through the program and read the biographies of the musicians.

After the symphony and on the way to the car Helen said, "Will you come up for a nightcap? I got us a surprise."

"A surprise? What is it?" Bel asked. She opened the car door for Helen.

"I went to the Cheesecake Factory this morning and picked us up one." Helen had gotten up early and picked out a good one. She wanted to please Bel.

Bel laughed. "Because we were fantasizing about cheesecake the other day?"

"Precisely. The psychological term for it is wish fulfillment. I also bought some amaretto."

Bel raised an eyebrow and started her black Lexus. "Horribly decadent."

"You can do extra laps on your treadmill at the gym. Not that you have an ounce of fat on you," Helen said. She pinched Bel's inner thigh.

"Ouch!" Bel said, feigning hurt. "I do have some fat."

"Sure."

"And I will be forced to do extra mileage to pay off the largesse of this evening." Helen gave her directions to her condo. Bel hadn't been there yet, since most of the time they met at Helen's office, which was located near Bel's law firm. Bel pulled into the parking lot of Helen's condo. They took the elevator up to the seventh floor.

"Come in. Let me take your jacket," Helen said. She took Bel's jacket and watched her go to the arcadia door to look out at the lights of Phoenix. Helen admired the beige silk button-down jacket. Bel had great taste in clothes and a pretty figure to go with it.

"Great view," Bel said, turning to face Helen.

"I bought it for that very reason. Plus the place is full of gay guys. They make the best neighbors. Ben, the guy next door, helped me decorate."

"It's nice. I like it," Bel said running her hand along the back of the deep brown leather couch.

"Ben's partner works for the Pottery Barn so we got some fantastic deals. I'm not much for artistic flair but those two are incredible. So I let them loose," Helen said, surveying the place again. It looked nothing like the placid, suburban home she had shared with Lars. Everything had been so neat, normal and nondescript. Here, there was funk, there was personality, there was a sense of what she was capable of—from the brightly colored rugs to the oak bookcases laced with odd artifacts. The place breathed of someone with fascinations outside herself, and Helen liked that. She poured them both a drink and then got out plates.

Bel eyed the cheesecake. "That looks fantastic."

"Wait until you taste it."

"Helen?"

"Yes?"

"Thank you for this evening."

"You're welcome, Bel. And don't worry if our daughters think it's weird we hang out so much."

Helen tasted the cheesecake. It was to die for, smooth but not overly heavy. She watched Bel.

"Well, what do you think?" Helen hoped Bel liked it as much as she did. It was if everything she did now outside of work seemed to revolve around Bel. When she would see her again, what she would wear and places they could go that Bel would like. This must be how a man feels when he courts a woman, she thought.

"Absolutely fabulous. You are now officially in charge of desserts."

Helen smiled, pleased.

Around midnight, Helen helped Bel on with her jacket. "You have great taste in perfume." Helen moved dangerously close to Bel's neck.

"Thank you," Bel said, turning toward her.

At that moment Helen heard God's voice in her head telling her, "She wants you to hold her." Helen, without thinking, obliged. She pulled Bel close and whispered, "I had a lovely time tonight."

Bel seemed flummoxed by the embrace. She said quickly, "So did I," and walked right into the closet door, obviously mistaking it for the front door.

"Are you all right?" Helen asked. She touched the red spot on Bel's forehead.

"Yes."

Helen ran her hand along Bel's cheek. "Let's get you out the correct door this time." She opened the front door. "Good night, Bel."

"Good night."

Helen shut the door and turned around to find God sitting on the couch looking rather smug.

"I don't think you should be coaching me."

"Someone has got to get the ball rolling. She loves you, and touching her cheek like that—very powerful."

"And all on my own, I might add," Helen said, going to the kitchen to put the dishes in the dishwasher. God followed.

"I don't get you women. It takes forever. A man gets a wiggle in his nether regions and it's straight to the bedroom. You women hem and haw, analyze and procrastinate until it's almost not worth it."

Helen laughed. "Bel is special to my heart and I don't want to mess this up for a simple roll in the hay. Besides, we're both straight, remember."

"Yeah, and I'm the frigging Pope. Since when did that ever stop any lesbian? Most of you start out straight and then bam, one day you go off into Vagina Land never to venture forth into Penis Land again. I got you pegged."

"I'm just saying that in time, if it became part of our relationship, I'm all right with that." She cut God a piece of cheesecake. She didn't appreciate God's eating it with her hands. "Here."

"This is marvelous."

"I'm glad you like it." Helen handed her a fork.

"So you would do her?" God said with her mouth full.

"That's rude."

"What, me talking with my mouth full or the comment?"

"Both."

"Who's the puritan now?" God asked. She wiped her chin on the napkin Helen handed her.

"She's special." Helen knew she was blushing, but lately when she thought about Bel she had these feelings of affection that she knew were a little too powerful for just a friendship.

"I know, and it'll all work out. You need to send those orchids."

"I know. I just thought she might think it odd getting flowers from another woman."

"She won't now. Can I have another piece?" God held up her plate.

"Sure. I'll send the flowers first thing Monday morning."

"Good."

After God left, Helen lay in bed replaying the evening in her head. She couldn't help wondering if Bel was having similar thoughts. It wasn't like she could ask her, so she kept looking for clues. It all seemed so ambiguous sometimes. And then there was the thing with God. Tonight, she had breached the ethics of her own profession. Doctors and patients weren't supposed to fraternize and tonight they had definitely done that. She supposed it would be difficult to bring her up on charges since God was technically an omnipresent being who was not subject to the same rules as the rest of the world. Besides, it would be most difficult to prove

God's existence. Of course, that's what she was treating God for. God felt like her identity was in jeopardy and she felt powerless to do anything about it. Even the Almighty had issues.

On Monday morning, Rafferty and Megan walked into Bel's office to find an enormous vase full of white orchids sitting on her desk. Bel had called them in to talk about the specifics of their latest case.

"What's this?" Rafferty asked, pointing to the orchids.

"They're lovely," Megan said.

"They appear to be orchids," Bel said. She got up to pull a leather-bound volume of legal precedents from the bookshelf behind her.

"Well, no shit," Rafferty said in an exasperated tone.

Megan smiled. She found Rafferty's lack of decorum amusing at times.

"Rafferty," her mother reprimanded.

"Sorry. Who sent them?"

"Someone special," Bel replied. Megan could tell she was trying to appear nonchalant.

"And who is that?" Rafferty said, plucking the card from the lovely white flowers.

"Rafferty, no. Please don't do that," Bel pleaded.

Megan watched as Rafferty studied the card and then looked at her mother. "It's private?" Rafferty said.

"Yes."

"Well, all right. Whoever it is has money and taste. He can't be all that bad," Rafferty said lightly. Megan knew Rafferty was playing it cool but underneath she was freaking. They had discussed their childhoods and the lack of men in them. Rafferty had told her that she'd been a total shit when her mother started dating again after her father died and that Bel had eventually given up, except for her friendship with Harold, whom Rafferty considered harmless.

"Thank you," Bel said. Bel took a deep breath and Megan suddenly knew who the flowers were from. She met Bel's gaze.

"It's all right, Bel," Megan said. She didn't know for certain if Bel got it that she knew the flowers were from her mother but it was kind of nice to see Bel a little bit frazzled. She was human after all.

"Okay, let's get down to business. I need you two to go to the law library and look up body parts, specifically, the removal of body parts from the recently deceased. You're probably going to have to go way back, but we're looking for a precedent," Bel said.

"Is this about the weirdo guy?" Rafferty asked.

"Rafferty, please refrain from using derogatory comments about our clients. Now, I want you two to actually go to the library. No stopping by the condo for a quickie. Got it?"

"Yes, Mother."

Out in the hall, Megan snatched Rafferty's hand and pulled her into the custodial storage closet. She kissed her ardently. "I need my midday fix," Megan said, stroking Rafferty's face.

"Ditto," Rafferty said, kissing her again.

"I love you," Megan whispered.

"No one could ever say those words the way you do."

"How did she find out about us playing hooky?" Megan asked. They'd only done it a few times, and as far as she was concerned, Saturdays didn't count.

"She's probably got my condo bugged."

"God, I hope not."

"What, you don't want my mother hearing you come into the wild blue yonder?"

"Exactly."

Just then, Sam, the janitor, opened the door. Megan and Rafferty giggled, straightened up and left for the law library.

❧

Later that evening, Helen drove her silver Honda Accord into Bel's circular driveway. She knew this time something was different, whether it was her woman's intuition or a few encouraging words from the big woman upstairs that had led her to this conclusion. Bel had called earlier in the day to thank her for the flowers and invite her to dinner. Helen was thrilled. She was also glad her palms were completely healed. She no longer needed the Band-Aids and only small scars remained.

"I thought we'd be totally decadent and have tenderloin medallions and lobster with a great bottle of wine and then finish off with chocolate mousse for desert," Bel had said.

"It sounds wonderful. Can I bring anything?"

"No, just your lovely self."

Of course Helen stopped and picked up something to bring. She decided on a box of horribly expensive Godiva chocolates. She would never splurge like that for herself but she could for Bel.

And now sitting in the driveway, Helen wondered if she and Bel would ever admit that they had feelings for each other. Would they go to that special place where they became lovers? Helen felt sure that many straight women had encountered similar epiphanies but quickly moved past them, never allowing themselves to go any further.

Helen went up to the front door and rang the bell. She was just a little nervous and hoped she wasn't blushing. Bel smiled widely when she saw her.

"What's this here?" Bel said, pointing to the square gold box of chocolates.

"I couldn't come empty-handed."

"Godiva are my favorites." Bel led her into the kitchen where pots were boiling and everything smelled fantastic.

"You know, I'm in absolute awe of your culinary skills," Helen said, taking a barstool at the large tiled kitchen island. Bel's kitchen was indicative of everything else in Bel's house—impeccable, tasteful, elegant and expensive. Helen looked around. Bel loved to cook, Helen knew, and she appeared to own every conceivable kitchen gadget, all stainless steel. The fridge and stove were also stainless steel. Helen admired the Viking six-burner stove. It smelled like chocolate coming from a double boiler that was poised on one of the six burners. A huge lobster pot was simmering on one of the back burners. Beautifully polished copper pans hung from a large rack overhead. Bel was wearing a high-collared white silk shirt and blue and white twill apron. Helen knew she would remember every aspect of this moment. It was as if they were both frozen in time. There was a soft glow in Bel's brown eyes.

"What?" Bel asked when she looked up to find Helen watching her. She was pouring them each a glass of red wine.

Helen smiled. "You look lovely."

"Dr. Kohlrabi, if I didn't know better I'd say you were flirting with me."

"I would never dream of compromising your integrity in such a manner," Helen said, taking the glass of Merlot that Bel offered her.

The buzzer on the oven went off and Bel turned toward the oven. She put the steaks on the broiler. She turned back around. "Were you flirting with me?" she asked, her face serious.

"If you wanted me to," Helen replied, equally serious. She could feel her heart rate increasing dramatically.

"I would hate to ruin a wonderful friendship . . ." Bel quickly starting whisking the chocolate on the stove.

Helen was crestfallen. They weren't going to that special place. This was as good as it got, she thought sadly.

"But I have these feelings that are a little more than just a friendship warrants, and I really don't know what to do about them or how you would feel if I told you."

Helen got up from the barstool and moved slowly toward Bel. Their gazes locked. Helen was afraid, but she knew it was this moment or never. She took the chance and wrapped her arms around Bel. "Tell me." Helen could feel Bel shaking.

"I don't know quite how to say this."

"Would you like to take this friendship a little further?" Helen prodded.

"Yes."

"So would I," Helen said, as she nuzzled Bel's neck.

The buzzer went off and the lobster pot was close to boiling over. Bel jumped as if startled from a dream. Helen kissed her forehead. "Let's have dinner and then we'll talk more."

Bel nodded. Helen had never seen her look so nervous and totally vulnerable. It made her want to scoop Bel up in her arms and kiss away all her fears.

"I bought a book," Bel said. She turned off the buzzer and readjusted the temperature of the stove.

"A book?"

"You know, in case we're at a loss."

"Oh, that kind of book."

"I thought we might look at it after dinner," Bel said shyly.

"Of course, my darling one," Helen said, sliding her arm around Bel's waist and kissing her cheek. Bel smiled. "See, that wasn't so hard."

"That was really hard," Bel said.

Dinner was fabulous. The lobster was cooked to perfection and the tenderloin medallions melted in your mouth. Bel had prepared a chef's salad and they had garlic bread.

Afterwards, Bel and Helen sat on the couch perusing a book of lesbian sex and erotica. Bel's head was cocked to one side.

"I don't think that's humanly possible," Helen said, puzzled by the line drawing they were studying.

"Only by a practiced contortionist."

"Bel?"

"Yes," Bel said, still studying the diagram.

"Maybe I could just kiss you and we could see where that takes us," Helen suggested.

"Skip the academics?"

"Precisely." Helen closed the book.

"All right," Bel said. She looked scared.

Helen took Bel's face in her hands and kissed Bel's forehead, then her closed eyes. She slowly kissed Bel's mouth. Their tongues touched and Bel moaned softly. Helen backed away. "How was that?"

"I'm not sure. Let's try it again," Bel said coyly.

"Bel!"

"I just want to be certain."

They kissed slow and long. Helen watched as the color rose in Bel's face. She kissed her neck and traced the outline of Bel's collarbone with her fingertip, then she unbuttoned the front of her shirt and reached for her breasts. This was fast but Helen couldn't help herself. Now that they'd gone here she had no intention of stopping. She cupped her hand around Bel's smooth breast. At this moment, she completely understood why men thought about sex constantly. All she wanted was Bel. She pulled off Bel's shirt and gently ran her index finger around Bel's nipple. Bel quivered.

"Are you okay?" Helen asked.

"Yes," Bel whispered in a throaty tone.

Helen pulled Bel on top of her. The wide leather couch made a near perfect twin bed. Helen could feel the heat between them as she kissed Bel.

Helen whispered, "I want to feel you."

Bel reached down and undid Helen's pants while Helen did the same to her. She ran her hand along Bel's butt and pulled her in closer. Helen could feel Bel's wetness and she moaned softly as Helen put her finger inside her.

"Oh, Bel." She reached for her and together they rocked against each other until Helen felt Bel come. She released moments later.

"I think we know what to do," Helen said, smiling up at Bel.

Bel laughed. They were lying in a tangle of clothes and the couch pillows lay scattered on the floor. "Wow," Bel said, rolling on her side.

"I hope you don't think I'm fast now," Helen said.

"No, but I would like to take you upstairs and treat you proper," Bel said. They stood up from the couch.

"You mean with all our clothes off beneath silk sheets."

"Precisely. How did you know I have silk sheets?"

"A woman like you has them."

Bel took Helen's hand and led her upstairs to the bedroom. She had a massive candelabra on her dresser. She lit the candles.

Helen sat down on the edge of the four-poster bed, which did have burgundy sheets. She took off the rest of her clothes and then she helped Bel do the same. "You have a lovely body." Helen ran her hand down Bel's flat stomach.

Bel eased her down on the bed and kissed her breasts. She kissed her stomach and kissed between Helen's legs. Helen felt Bel's tongue slide between inner lips and she moaned softly. When she felt Bel's tongue on her clitoris, her breathing grew ragged. Then Bel turned her on her stomach and took her from behind. Helen ground against her and reached for Bel who positioned herself so Helen could be inside her. They both came within seconds of each other.

"My God, Bel, I think you've studied that book more than you let on," Helen said. She unfurled her hand from the sheet. Bel still lay across her back.

"I wanted to please you."

"I don't think I've ever felt like that before."

Bel laughed. "You and me both. You know, for the first time in my life, I think I understand where Rafferty is coming from."

Chapter Ten

On Tuesday morning Megan met Rafferty in the conference room. They were waiting for Bel to give her an update on the new case involving the display of body parts. Megan frowned at the thin layer of dust that covered the dark cherry-wood table. Sam should have cleaned it. She grabbed a paper towel from the restroom and wiped it off while Rafferty sat in one of the executive swivel chairs and stared out the window.

"What is going on around here?" Megan asked. Rafferty had been distracted all morning. It appeared she was obsessed with Bel's secret lover. Megan had tried to get her to talk about her feelings but Rafferty would have none of it, so Megan had let it go.

"What do you mean?" Rafferty said, swiveling back around.

"You went to get coffee and then didn't get any. Sam is upset because Bel came down on him and he still isn't cleaning the place, and now you're in some weird kind of funk. I can tell," Megan said, putting her hands on her hips.

Rafferty shrugged.

Megan spied Sam go by in the hallway. "Hey, Sam, can I have a word?"

"Sure, what's up?" Sam said, pulling a rag from his back pocket.

Megan smiled. "Is the rag for looks or are you actually going to do some work with it?"

"Excuse me?" Sam said.

"Look at this place," Megan said, pointing to the swipe on the conference table where she had attempted to clean.

"Who did that? They didn't do a very good job."

Bel came around the corner and entered the room.

"I did. It's filthy in here, Sam. See, the deal is, we're lawyers and we do, you know, law things, and you're Sam, our beloved cleaning guy. So the law people would like to sit at a clean table that Sam, the cleaning guy, was supposed to have cleaned," Megan said.

"Right," Sam said. He took his rag and thoroughly dusted the table, studiously avoiding Bel's gaze although she wasn't paying the least bit of attention, Megan noticed.

"I brought your coffee. You forgot it," Bel said, setting the cup in front of Rafferty.

"Thanks," she said sullenly.

Megan waited until Sam was through and then she shut the door behind him. "All right, now that that's settled, perhaps we can get some work done." She turned around to find both Bel and Rafferty staring out the window. "What the hell is going on here?" Megan said, frustrated.

Bel and Rafferty both swiveled around to stare at her blankly.

"The Mackowski file, the guy who keeps all his dead wife's organs in the front window of his house, that guy, the one the homeowners' association is threatening to sue for some big bucks if we can't convince the nut job to change his ways," Megan huffed. The homeowners' association was a long-term client of theirs.

"I think that's pretty evident," Rafferty said. "He's not exactly running a natural history museum."

"We're going to need more than anecdotal evidence from his

lawyer that keeping the various organs his wife had removed over the years due to cancer is normal behavior," Megan replied.

"Perhaps we could have Helen talk to him about expressions of grief, appropriate expressions of grief. People do odd things when they're grieving," Bel suggested.

Megan liked the idea but wondered about the ethics of it. "What about conflict of interest? She is my mother."

"If it comes down to it, which it shouldn't, we'll have Rafferty plead the case. Lord knows she's dispassionate. Rafferty thinks he's a nut job and her belief will run over nicely onto the judge," Bel said.

"My mother says the human psyche is an unfathomable place," Megan said, pulling out the file.

"Great, so I'm going to get all the nut-job cases," Rafferty said, taking a sip of her coffee.

"Look, the association is a good client. They want a normal neighborhood and it's our job to see they get it. They want the man and his body parts to go away but he's within his rights to keep them, so buck up," Bel said.

"So let me get this straight—you do bad clergy, Megan does slick businesspeople and I do whack jobs."

"It's an unpleasant world, Rafferty. But without those kind of people the world wouldn't need lawyers," Bel said. She took her copy of the brief from Megan.

"So I'll see what my mother can do."

"Don't bother. I'm having a late lunch with her this afternoon," Bel said.

Rafferty sat up straight in her chair.

"Great, you can tell us what we need to do when you get back from lunch?" Megan shuffled through the stack of documents in front of her. "He had an evaluation when they held him for disturbing the peace when the home association first started the complaint. I know it's here somewhere."

"What, someone threatened to take his jars away?" Rafferty said snidely.

"Something like that," Megan said, preoccupied with her papers.

"I'm not coming back," Bel said, studying the stack of papers in front of her and avoiding their gaze.

"And why is that?" Rafferty inquired.

"Because we have plans," Bel said.

"What sort of plans?" Rafferty said, staring hard at her mother.

"Girl things. Helen is taking a half-day off. If that's all right with you. Now, did you find that evaluation?"

"Like shopping?" Rafferty said.

"Something like that. Now, can we get on with this?" Bel snapped.

After work Rafferty helped Megan carry out a box of depositions she was going to work on that evening. "I don't know how we're going to have any fun when you have all this work to do."

"You're going to help me. That'll cut the time in half. Look, all we have to do is catalogue them and put them in some kind of useable order. The rest we can work on tomorrow."

"Oh, goody. Isn't that what clerks are for?"

"I'll make it worth your time," Megan said. She put her thigh between Rafferty's legs as Rafferty struggled with the box and attempted to find her keys. She moaned softly.

"Can't we put these in the trunk?" Megan asked.

"No, it's full of stuff."

"What kind of stuff?" Megan watched as Rafferty attempted to shove the box in the back seat.

"Things."

"Rafferty, when are you going to tell me about your secret life?"

"What are you talking about?"

"The dirt on your shoes, the muddy tires on your car, the calluses on your hands. Why don't you tell me where you go sometimes in the middle of the afternoon?"

Rafferty was quiet.

"Are you afraid I'll laugh or want you to stop what you're doing?"

"No."

"Then what?"

"It's private."

"Let me guess, you're some kind of rustic camp S and M instructor."

"No."

"Okay, you're a calf roper."

"Closer."

"Come on, what? We're supposed to sharing our lives, not just our bodies."

"All right." Rafferty unlocked the trunk.

Megan peered inside to find a saddle, ropes, a set of bright red cowboy boots and several pairs of Wrangler jeans. She pulled a pair out and held them up. "Oh, baby, I bet you look hot in these."

"Give me those," Rafferty said, snatching the jeans back and shoving them back into the trunk.

"So where's the ranch?"

"You really want to see it?"

"I really want to see the Wranglers but I'm willing to go sightseeing."

"Megan!"

"Come on, let's go. I want to know all about your secret life."

"Promise not to tell?"

"I promise."

They got into the car and Megan dug around in Rafferty's CD collection that was strewn all over the car.

"What are you looking for?"

"Some Lyle Lovett. I want to get into the mood of this cowgirl thing."

"As a matter of fact, I do have one or two." Rafferty pulled it out of her glove box.

"No way, really."

"Yup." She shoved the disc in the player and then pulled a straw cowboy hat from the depths of the backseat. Rafferty's car was always a mess. "This might help."

Megan stuck the hat on and then checked herself out in the rearview mirror.

"You look good." Rafferty smiled for the first time all day.

Rafferty drove them out of Phoenix and toward a small town called Wickenburg. Megan had heard of it, a small town whose primary revenue came from the prison located nearby. Megan loved the desert with its giant saguaro cactus, dark green leaves of the creosote tree and the grappling prickly pear with its purple fruit hanging like Christmas tree balls. When she was a child and they had first moved to Phoenix from Chicago she had picked one up in the neighbor's yard and came home screaming, her tiny hands full of cactus spikes. Helen had to take her to the emergency room to have them removed. Her mother hated cactus plants from that moment on and Megan had grown up in the only house on the block with a green lawn. All the other yards were rocky and filled with desert flora. Megan had been forbidden to go anywhere near a native plant. This, of course, made them all the more intriguing.

"I forget how pretty the desert is," Megan said as she took Rafferty's hand.

"And peaceful," Rafferty replied. She turned onto a dirt road.

Megan rocked in her seat as the pearl-white Miata bumped along the washboard road.

"So where is this place?"

"Up the road a few miles," Rafferty said.

Megan noticed her eyes getting glassy. "This makes you really happy, doesn't it?"

"Very happy."

"Did you always want to be a cowgirl?" Megan asked as she ran her finger around the hard callus on Rafferty's finger.

"Absolutely."

"What stopped you?"

"The law."

"What, the town sheriff told you being a cowgirl was a no-no?"

"Not exactly. The law, as in my mother."

"She wouldn't let you?"

"I never asked but she wouldn't have agreed. It's not a proper profession," Rafferty said, turning into the ranch.

Megan glanced up at the huge metal sign that hung overhead. It read *The Lone Girl Ranch*. "Great name. Hey, it's for sale," Megan said, pointing at the realty sign.

"I know," Rafferty said, looking at the sign mournfully.

"You could buy it."

"I couldn't afford the mortgage."

"How much?"

"Just a cool million."

"Ouch!"

"It's a hundred and forty acres, has four horse barns, a massive house and four guest houses, and most of the horses stay."

"Wow! That's a deal. Why are they selling?"

"Flo, the owner, is seventy. She says the place needs young blood." Rafferty pulled into one of the parking lots by barn number four. "This is where I board them."

"Board them?"

"Lighting and Thunderbolt. They're two mares, one white and one gray and both absolutely beautiful."

"You're talking like a proud parent."

"I am."

"They don't sound like slow horses."

"They're not." Rafferty smiled as if secretly proud.

"And Bel knows nothing about it?" Megan said, taking the bridles and blankets that Rafferty handed her.

"Nothing, and I expect it to stay that way."

"My lips are sealed."

Rafferty led Megan into the cool darkness of the horse barn. The smell of hay infiltrated her senses. Megan watched as Rafferty approached her horses, who took turns nuzzling her. She stroked Lightning's brilliant white coat. Thunderbolt nuzzled her way in. Rafferty stroked her nose.

"Wow, she's a big horse," Megan said.

"And she can be quite testy. Lightning, on the other hand, is very sweet and will do anything I tell her." She gave them each a carrot.

The horses neighed and Rafferty put on their bridles. She led them all to the fenced area just outside the barn. Lightning pulled at the bridle and came close to Megan.

Megan held out her hand and Lightning dipped down her head so she could stroke the beautiful white mare's forehead.

"I guess she's yours now. It appears she's been waiting for you to show up," Rafferty said.

"Really?"

"I got them both hoping one day I'd have someone to share them with."

"I don't know how to ride."

"You will."

Rafferty saddled up the horses and helped Megan get on. Lightning sat perfectly still while Megan tried to get settled. Then Rafferty opened the gate and they went out onto the open plains around the ranch. Megan still had her cowboy hat on and by the end of their ride she was doing pretty well. Rafferty smiled at her in the same way as when she had learned to fish. Lightning was a great horse and Megan patted her forehead and looked back longingly as they left. "When do we get to come back?"

"Soon. We've got to get through this nut job with the jar fetish first," Rafferty said. Megan didn't stop smiling the whole way home.

Up on the hill God and Gigi had stood watching them ride. Two women racing across the desert landscape looked happier than Gigi had seen two people look, other than Caroline's face this morning after Gigi had ardently seduced her. It seemed relationships weren't as hard as Gigi once imagined them. She bought flowers, made dinner, made love and behaved nicely to Caroline, which seemed to make her horribly happy. Gigi didn't scope other women, came home on time and Caroline loved her.

"So those are the women we're sharing the ranch with?" Gigi asked.

"Yes, their names are Megan and Rafferty. Megan is Dr. Kohlrabi's daughter."

"Hot chick, she never told me."

"Nor would she ever," God said, adjusting her silver belt buckle. It was a big as a dessert plate. She was dressed in a plaid cowboy shirt and Wranglers with red cowboy boots and a straw hat.

"Why don't you just let them have the ranch? Horses make me nervous. I'm kind of an urban girl," Gigi said, watching them ride off. Megan and Rafferty had stopped for a minute, probably wondering what two women were doing out in the middle of nowhere with no apparent transportation anywhere in sight. Gigi couldn't explain it either. She had lain down for a nap after work and next thing she knew she was in the middle of a ranch.

"That's not part of the plan. People will come here because you're here and besides, you'll need each other, trust me."

"So this thing doesn't end with the book then?"

"That is correct," God said, leaning over and plucking a long piece of grass. She stuck it between her lips. "Isn't this place grand?" she said as she looked out over the horizon.

"Yeah, it's great if you're into that kind of thing," Gigi said.

"You'll learn to like it."

"Like I have a choice," Gigi muttered. "By the way, Randolph has stepped up production just like you asked so the book will be out by the end of summer. He says your punctuation is amazing. This is the best book he's ever edited. I think he's a little paranoid about editing the word of God."

"As well he should be."

Gigi smiled. It appeared God's feathers were a bit ruffled over that last remark. "In the beginning was the word . . ."

"Exactly. All right, let's go."

"Good, I'm supposed to be napping."

"You will be in a minute."

Wednesday afternoon, Bel, Rafferty and Megan met with the homeowners' association board. They were nice enough people living in an upscale development who did not want some grief-stricken man to display pickled body parts in his front window. It was a reasonable enough request, Megan thought.

"So, we've got a compromise solution," Bel told them.

"Which is?" a large woman wearing a horrible floral dress that looked like it should have been someone's drapes asked snidely.

Bel gave Megan a pregnant look. This one's going to be a hard sell, her look seemed to say. Megan smiled nicely and explained the plan. "We get Mr. Mackowski to agree to remove the jars from the front window and put them in a curio cabinet. He still gets to keep them but they're out of sight, and he gets some grief counseling to better help him deal with the loss of his wife, whom he dearly loved."

"But they're still in the house," said a small, thin man with black-rimmed glasses who was holding hands with the large woman. He appeared to be her husband.

Rafferty started to say something but Megan kicked her under the table.

"Technically speaking, there's no law against having body parts in your house. Ask any child harboring their lost baby teeth. Look, we just want to reach a compromise here. It's going to be difficult to convince a judge to evict Mr. Mackowski. It's a property rights issue and it could be a very timely and costly task to get this done. Besides, he shouldn't have to lose his house because he thinks these things in jars are all he has left of his wife. Let him get some counseling and he'll probably end up getting rid of them anyway. Just give him some time," Megan said.

A mousy woman sitting at the end of the table burst into tears. "That's so beautiful. I never thought of it that way." She pulled a Kleenex from her white patent-leather purse.

"So why don't you all think about it and get back to us next week. You know, going to court is not really much fun. It just looks intriguing on television," Bel said.

The group agreed and Bel showed them out. When she returned, Rafferty was banging her head on the conference table.

"Those have got to be the most petty, stupid people I've ever met," Rafferty said.

"They did look like they were out of some bad sitcom," Bel said. They both started to laugh.

Megan smiled.

"You, however, did a great job of selling the proposal," Bel told Megan.

"I thought I did a pretty good job of keeping my mouth shut, because if you only knew what I was thinking," Rafferty said.

"Which is exactly why we didn't let you talk," Megan said.

By Friday, the homeowners' association had agreed to the curio cabinet idea. Megan had gone shopping with Mr. Mackowski to find a curio cabinet because the whole prospect had him rather flummoxed. The mousy woman had brought him over a casserole and was going to drive him to counseling since he didn't drive. It appeared Mr. Mackowski was petrified of anything mechanical.

"Okay, so the guy's got some issues," Megan said as she straightened out her desk. They were going riding tomorrow and she could hardly wait. Rafferty was taking her shopping for some jeans and cowboy boots so she was in a hurry to get out of there.

"Issues? The guy is a complete nut job," Rafferty said.

Bel popped in. "Have a good weekend, girls."

"Hey, Mom, what are you doing this weekend?"

"Oh, just some stuff around the house." Megan noticed Bel didn't look at Rafferty.

Something's afoot, Megan thought. Bel seemed a little too happy about just hanging around the house. She tried to distract Rafferty. "Are you ready?"

"Sure, see you later, Mom."

Chapter Eleven

On Friday night after dinner, Helen watched as Bel drew the blinds and cranked up the air conditioner so Bel's house would get a good chill. Helen shivered. Then Bel started a fire in the den.

"I always thought it was absurd that a house would have a fireplace when it's so damn hot here all the time, but it makes the room," Bel said, indicating the heavy cherrywood mantel and granite hearth in front of the large fireplace. The rest of the den was furnished with cherrywood bookcases, soft brown leather chairs and matching couch along with a large red oriental rug in the center of the room.

"I love this room," Helen said, sitting down on the rug in front of the fireplace. She sipped her wine.

Bel put more wood on the fire and then sat down next to Helen. "I love you, you know that," she said, her face serious.

"Of course I do." Helen stroked Bel's cheek. "And the feeling is mutual." She put her wineglass on the end table, looked at Bel and said, "I've always had this thing about fireplaces and . . ." She stopped, unsure if she wanted to go on.

"And?" Bel prodded.

"Well, you know."

"No, I don't."

Helen smiled. "Why do I get the idea that you're teasing me?"

"Because I am. Tell me what you want."

"I just always thought it would be nice to have a seduction scene in front of a fireplace with someone special. I know it sounds corny but . . ." Helen blushed and lowered her eyes.

Bel caught her chin and raised her head so their gazes met. "Why do you think we're having a fire?"

"Oh, Bel," Helen said as Bel eased her down on her back and kissed her softly.

Early Saturday morning, Megan awoke to find Rafferty sitting on the bed next to her. She was fully dressed. "Rafferty, what the hell time is it?" She squinted at the clock. "Six?"

They had stayed up late watching a movie, drinking beer and eating pizza in bed. It was utter decadence, followed by ardent lovemaking. Six in the morning felt like the crack of dawn. Megan wanted to go horseback riding, but nine would be fine.

"It's six. You can sleep more. I want to go talk to my mom."

"About what?"

"Just to visit," Rafferty said, not meeting Megan's gaze.

"At this ungodly hour? Rafferty, what's really going on?" Megan leaned up on one elbow.

"It's this secret love affair thing she has going on. I want to talk to her about it and I can't do it at the office. I'm going to pick us up some Starbucks coffee and have a little chat. It's not like her to keep secrets and I'm worried."

"She's a big girl."

"I know but this is big. I'll be back before you know it," Rafferty said. She kissed Megan's forehead.

"Don't get in a fight." Megan could tell Rafferty wasn't going to be dissuaded. She rolled back over and closed her eyes.

Upstairs at Bel's house that same morning, Bel lay on Helen's stomach. "I love you."

Helen smiled and ran her fingers through Bel's hair. "And I love you madly."

"No one has ever made me feel this way."

"What way is that?" Helen asked as she pulled Bel up closer until she held her in her arms.

"So well loved," Bel said, tears welling up in eyes.

Helen wiped Bel's eyes. "Thank you for taking us to this place. I don't think I would have had the courage even though I wanted to."

"I can honestly say that I've never had such a feeling of elation coupled with fear in my entire life as I did when I kissed you."

"I'm so glad you did."

Bel pulled her close. "Are you hungry?"

"Absolutely famished. It must be all the exercise."

"I bought you a present." Bel went to the closet and pulled out a beautifully wrapped present.

"What's this?" Helen asked. She unwrapped the present to find a black silk kimono with a small, very intricate dragon on the right breast. "It's beautiful. Thank you, Bel."

"I thought you might need it around here."

"So this is my first possession for your house?"

"Yes, and I hope there will be many more."

Helen put the robe on. "Oh, Bel, it's beautiful." She gave Bel a big hug.

"It looks great on you," Bel said, getting up and putting on her own silk robe. "I thought we'd have eggs Benedict."

"That sounds fabulous. Can we go like this?"

"Of course. Besides, your clothes are still downstairs."

Helen smiled.

They held hands as they went downstairs. As they rounded the corner, they both stopped in their tracks. Rafferty stood in the kitchen waiting for them. Helen watched Rafferty's face as recognition and disbelief took hold. This was not good, nor was it the way Helen had envisioned telling the girls. She had thought they'd have dinner, sit on the couch and have a rational chat about the nature of love and go from there.

"Helen?" Rafferty said. "What are you two doing?"

"I think that's fairly obvious. What are you doing here?" Bel asked.

"I came to talk to you, to see what's been going on in your life and why you've been so secretive."

"Not secretive, rather I've been private."

"But this . . . this isn't right. What are you doing? Helen is Megan's mother," Rafferty said, her face getting red.

"I'm aware of that," Bel said calmly.

"So is Megan next on your list of just-turned-lesbian conquests? Couldn't you have chosen someone else?"

"When you find your soul mate it's not a matter of choice," Bel replied.

"I can't believe you. You're sleeping with my girlfriend's mother," Rafferty screamed.

"Rafferty, stop it this minute," Bel said firmly. "I admit this is difficult but I love Helen and she just happens to be Megan's mother."

"That's great! Maybe we could all get a duplex and live together in mother-daughter harmony."

"Rafferty, you will cease this diatribe immediately and leave the premises until you've managed to control yourself and behave in a civilized manner," Bel said, taking control of the situation.

"Fine! Don't expect me back," she said. She slammed the front door.

"Like I want you to, you selfish brat!" Bel screamed after her.

Helen could see Bel had had enough. Bel banged her head on the doorframe and Helen put an arm around her shoulder. Helen refrained from telling her people in the loony bin exhibited similar behavior.

Bel looked over at Helen. "I certainly hope Megan takes it better."

"I think Megan may already know," Helen replied.

"You do?"

"Call it mother's intuition but she's dropped hints. Let me call her. If anyone can talk to Rafferty it's Megan."

"Somebody's got to. That child will be the death of me."

"I hope not."

Helen called Megan and explained the situation. Megan didn't seem surprised. "I thought she was up to something," Megan said, referring to Rafferty.

"What do you mean?" Helen asked.

"She was real secretive and said she'd be back shortly but it was like she needed to check on something. I guess we all figured that out. Did they get in a fight?"

"Yes."

"She didn't see you doing it, did she? Because that would've been truly traumatic."

"Megan! No, of course not."

"Good. I'll go find her and have a talk. Tell Bel not to worry. I've got the goods on Rafferty."

"Goods?"

"Leverage."

"So you're all right with this?"

"Well, yeah. It's kind of weird but I think Bel is hot and I want you to be happy. Besides, if Lars, the man who pretends to be my father, ever finds out, he'll freak. How cool is that? Maybe I'll send him a card, like the lame ones he sends me for my birthday."

Helen sighed. "Megan . . ."

"Sorry. I'll talk to Rafferty and try and fix things. I love you, Mom."

"I love you too." She hung up the phone and put on the coffee.

Bel let out an exasperated sigh and banged her head on the doorframe again. "How come your kid is so marvelous and mine is such a shit?"

"Megan thinks you're hot."

"I always liked that girl. So she knew?"

"Yes, I guess we weren't as discreet as we thought. It was bound to come out sooner or later."

"I would've preferred later."

Helen smiled and wrapped her arms around Bel. "This will all work out."

Bel nestled in Helen's arms. "God, I hope so."

Megan called Rafferty's cell phone in the vain hope that she might answer. Instead she got her voice mail. Rafferty had changed her message. It said, "I don't give a fuck who you are or what you want so don't bother leaving a fucking message."

Megan got out of bed and made coffee. Rafferty would show when she was ready. She spent the time trying to come up with a logical lawyer-like defense for her mother and Bel. Megan couldn't say she hadn't seen it coming, but clearly this wasn't something rash they had rushed into. In her opinion, they had slowly come to the conclusion that they were in love, and love, as she knew, had a physical side to it when you're consenting adults. Why Rafferty couldn't see this was beyond her. It was after all their story. Hadn't Megan come to the same kind of conclusion? Perhaps it was every woman's story who crosses the line that divides straight and gay.

Megan had just gotten out of the shower when Rafferty showed. She had stopped at McDonald's and gotten them breakfast. Megan took this to be a good sign. "Are you all right?"

"Your mother called you," Rafferty said, not meeting Megan's gaze.

"Yes."

"My mother's a coward."

"No, she's your mother and she's concerned about you." Megan poured two cups of coffee and got plates out for breakfast.

"If she was concerned about me she wouldn't be sleeping with your mother."

"Rafferty, love is a strange thing. Two months ago I was getting married and now I'm madly in love with you. Can't we give them a break? They probably had no idea that they would fall in love, but they did. You've got to cut them some slack."

"It's not that simple."

"Why are you so angry?"

Rafferty looked at Megan. "She could've told me. Instead, I have to sneak around and try and figure out what's going on. This is big and she didn't share it with me."

"That's why you're angry," Megan said, suddenly getting it. Rafferty felt left out and for the first time in her life she had been supplanted by someone else in her mother's affections. Megan put her arm around Rafferty's shoulders and whispered in her ear, "It's time you cut the cord. It's possible, you know, that Bel had similar feelings about falling in love."

"She never said anything."

"Nor would she. For as close a relationship as you two have, you don't communicate very well."

Rafferty smiled. "No, we don't."

"Come on, let's go riding and have a good day. This thing will work its way out. You've got to give your mom a chance."

"You really want to go?"

"I've got the outfit, don't I? I want to be a part of your passion, and since we both know it's horses and not the law, I need to learn about horses."

"You're amazing."

"Why?"

"Because you can take the worse moment and make it better."

After they ate breakfast and drove out to the ranch, Megan knew that her girlfriend would survive the first shock of cutting the cord with her mother. She knew there would be more but they would seem small in comparison.

On Monday morning, Rafferty and Megan attempted to cruise by Bel's office without being noticed. They were not successful.

"Rafferty and Megan, a word, please," Bel called out.

"Do I have to?" Rafferty said. Megan pinched her.

"Yes, please close the door."

Megan knew this was serious. Part of her wished she didn't have to be a part of it but the other part of her knew that this thing involved all of them and she had to hold up her end. Rafferty shut the door. Megan took a deep breath and prayed for the best. Bel sat on the corner of her desk.

"Rafferty, I know this is hard for you but the day I found you in the arms of the softball team captain was not an easy moment for me either. I was anxious, annoyed and concerned for your future. I know that love and sex are too important to be subjugated to the constrictions of gender. If you loved women, then I accepted that. I have a chance now to know happiness with Helen. Are you going to begrudge me that?"

"You had your chance with Dad."

"Your father was a prick. I prayed every day that God would take him and finally he did. The day he died was one of the happiest days of my life."

Megan watched as Rafferty stood staring in complete and utter disbelief. This was a bigger moment than she had envisioned. Rafferty had talked about her father in rather glowing terms and Megan had chalked it off as a young girl's vision of her dead father. She had told Rafferty about her father and how memory can distort things but it had not affected her. Megan let it stand. Rafferty was only six when her father died.

"Why did you stay if you hated him so much?"

"Your father was a very powerful man. If I had left him, he would have taken you away and made certain that I never had access to you. Besides, do you have any idea what he would have done with you and your homosexuality? You'd be locked up in a loony bin somewhere."

Rafferty was quiet. Megan could tell her whole make-believe world was crashing around her feet. Megan knew that Rafferty had few memories of her father so she had most likely concocted all sorts of girlish fantasies about what he was like. Megan had gone through a similar period when she'd told herself her father was not the terrible man who had deserted her mother and her to start up with a woman half his age. That lasted until the day she'd been assigned to a divorce case with similar circumstances and she had finally seen her father for what he was, a vain man in search of physical conquests. That day, the house of cards came crashing down.

"He wasn't like I imagined him."

"No, sweetie, he wasn't. He was a bad man that I protected you from."

"Do we have to go on family vacations?"

Bel laughed. "No."

"You know I like Helen. I just kind of freaked out."

"And became a raving homophobe."

"It was parental homophobia," Rafferty said.

"I know it's difficult and I admit it kind of blows my mind but I have never felt this happy, except for one day," Bel said, gazing out the window.

"When was that?" Rafferty said.

"The first time I saw you and held you in my arms."

"I was probably wailing up a storm too. You should have known then."

Bel pinched her arm and Megan laughed.

"Ouch!"

"You're so emotionally detached sometimes I wonder if you're even warm-blooded."

"Megan thinks differently," Rafferty said, staring intently at Megan.

"I bet she does, and you two need to behave yourselves. Sam keeps complaining about finding you two popping out of his utility closet."

"I love you, Mom."

Bel pulled her close.

Chapter Twelve

Helen was in her office Friday morning talking to God, who was still having an identity crisis that Helen couldn't seem to cure her of. God, it seemed, believed that the world had forgotten the original nature of her being and was instead entertaining notions that even God couldn't have come up with and too much of it was filled with distortions and hatred. Helen nodded sadly.

"You have no solution?" God said, rubbing her sweaty palms on her khaki Capri pants. She was wearing a Hawaiian print shirt with giant blue and yellow flowers on it and a pair of Birkenstocks. She looked like the epitome of a tourist, which Helen supposed she was.

"I think writing your book was a good idea. I don't understand the new title. Why *The Gossamer Effect*?"

God picked up the Buddha statue and petted his little bald head. "Have I ever told you the story of filament?"

"Excuse me?" Helen wondered if the story was somehow connected to the title of the book. The longer she hung out with God the more she understood the reasoning behind the tangential nature of the universe. God was one big tangent.

"It's the story of gossamer wings," God said, putting the statue back on the desk.

"What are you talking about?"

"It's the idea that the world as you know it is covered in an invisible film like a giant spider web that connects us all. As one person behaves so it affects the lives and behavior of others but sometimes it takes a shove to get the whole thing going."

"Thus the gossamer wings." Helen liked it when things came to neat conclusions, especially when they pertained to God.

"Precisely, because sometimes it can go stagnant and lose its flexibility. This doesn't happen if it keeps moving." God fluttered her fingers to illustrate her point.

"I think the title is pertinent. Perhaps what needs to happen is an incremental reintroduction of faith and kindness back into the universe. The book will be a start."

"I'm glad you feel that way, because there's a second part to my idea."

"What might that be?" Helen felt her heart beat more rapidly. Somehow this was going to involve her. The other thing that she had noticed about spending time with God was that God always had ulterior motives.

"You're having Megan and Rafferty for dinner on Sunday, correct?"

"Yes, how did you know? Oh, never mind."

God smiled.

"I can't get used to the idea that you know everything."

"I'd like to come for dinner."

"Oh?" Helen wondered what this was about.

"I need to talk to Megan and Rafferty. I have a little assignment for them."

"What kind of an assignment?" Now Helen's palms were sweating. They were completely healed, so whatever strange skin disorder they had suffered was in the process of correcting itself. Helen was convinced God was somehow involved in the healing process. Gigi's mother had sprinkled holy water on her feet and they were now good as new. Helen remembered Gigi telling her the story of her mother sending away for holy water. Rose had made them pray together and then doused Gigi's feet with the stuff. It appeared to have worked. Gigi thought her mother was completely nuts but she didn't complain about the results.

"Rafferty boards her horses at a ranch that's for sale."

"She has horses?"

"No one but Megan knows this. I need them to buy the ranch."

"Why?"

"It's located on a vortex. Gigi and the girls will run it as a dude ranch. This will be a disguise for its true purpose. Certain people will be drawn here, where they'll change and then go back into the world to keep the gossamer effect going."

"That is the most absurd scheme I've ever heard of," Helen said, hoping she might stand some chance of talking God out of her new plan. This was unprofessional of her, she knew, but for the sake of family harmony she was willing to step out of character.

"Which is precisely why it will work," God said adamantly.

Helen shook her head. "It's ludicrous. None of them has that kind of money."

"No, but they will," God said, smiling.

When God smiled like that, it always made Helen nervous. It meant she was up to something. "How?" she asked.

"A well-timed, well-placed bet."

"On the horses?" Helen said, suddenly catching on. "Bel's going to kill me."

"No, she won't. She loves you. But she's going to be perfectly furious with me. It will, however, strengthen her relationship with Rafferty. She'll be happier being a cowgirl and Bel will still have

Megan, whom she'll groom to be a great lawyer. Everyone will be happier."

"As soon as Bel gets over the shock," Helen replied.

"Well, yes, there is that small detail."

"How can you be certain this plan will work?"

"Because where there's a dream, there's passion, and that combination renders the impossible a nonentity. In ten thousand years I've discovered that small revolutions work better than one big one."

"You've done this before?"

God smiled. "Now, about dinner."

On Sunday evening, Bel was cooking up a storm in the kitchen. There was food everywhere on the kitchen island and pots all over the stove. "I can't believe she's coming for dinner," Bel said. Her face was flushed and her temples were wet. Helen couldn't decide if Bel was sweating from cooking or having a panic attack. Most likely it was the latter.

"Yes, well, it is rather unusual. I think the roux is burning," Helen said, pointing to the saucepan on the stove. Bel whipped around.

"Oh, shit!" She pulled the pan off the stove.

Megan and Rafferty had arrived earlier and were setting the large dining room table with explicit instructions from Bel. Rafferty came sauntering in the kitchen. Bel grabbed her by the shoulders. "We have a very important guest coming for dinner. You are not to be smart, provocative, or get out of line in any manner or fashion. You're to do everything she says. Do you understand?"

Rafferty was clearly shocked by Bel's firm tone.

"Do you want to spend the rest of your life in hell?"

"No."

"Then do it."

"Yes, ma'am." Rafferty looked to Helen for guidance.

"She's just a little nervous," Helen said, going over and rubbing Bel's shoulders. "It's going to be all right. Now take a deep breath and remember you are a great cook, God loves food and Rafferty will behave herself."

Bel relaxed a little.

"Now, what can I do to help. I'm a great prep cook."

"You can make the salad. Everything's right there." Bel handed her a chef's knife and got out a large crystal bowl.

God slipped in the back door. Both Helen and Bel jumped as God peered over Bel's shoulder at the wild rice and mushroom soup.

"It smells fantastic," God said, taking a big sniff.

"You almost gave me a heart attack," Bel said, putting her hand to her chest.

"I would have saved you," God said sweetly.

"She's a little nervous about cooking you dinner," Helen explained. Her pulse was racing. She knew from this moment on their lives were going to change dramatically. She felt guilty for not telling Bel about God's latest plan, but she was bound by doctor-patient confidentiality. Plus she'd been advised by God to keep her mouth shut. One did not argue with the Almighty. God's threatening Gigi with the lightning bolt still stuck firm in Helen's mind.

God peered into the dining room. "Where's Rafferty?"

"I sent her down to the wine cellar," Bel said. "Please tell me that you'll forgive any of her transgressions this evening."

"Relax, everything will be fine."

"I hate trying to figure out your insane system of organizing that place," Rafferty mumbled as she ascended the stairs.

God took the bottle of wine from her. "Good year."

"Hey, long time no see," Rafferty said with a smile.

"You remember?"

"Of course. I actually cried when you left," Rafferty said. "That's big for me."

"Yeah, it is," God said. "I told you I'd be back."

Bel stood there stunned. "You know each other?"

"She was my imaginary friend," Rafferty said matter-of-factly.

"She was Delphi?" Bel said.

"A rather fitting name, I thought," God said smugly.

"I always thought you were the one who ate the extra snack you insisted I put out for your friend and I was afraid you were going to get fat. I never understood why a six-year-old insisted on pickled herring and black coffee."

"Thanks. You made great cracker plates. The pickled herring was my favorite," God said, rubbing her belly.

"Hey, that trick with the plants was hilarious."

"I thought you'd appreciate it," God said.

Megan came in.

"Megan, I'd like you to meet Delphi," Rafferty said, winking at God.

"So nice to meet you," God said, extending her hand.

Megan shook her hand. "Rafferty, wasn't that the name of your imaginary friend?"

"As a matter of fact . . ."

"Rafferty, perhaps you should get us another bottle of wine," Bel interjected.

"But I was just down there."

"Take Megan with you," Bel suggested.

"All right," Rafferty said, getting a gleam in her eye. "What kind now?"

"You pick," Bel replied.

After they left, Bel whipped around. "You're going to get us all burned at the stake at this rate."

"Relax, Bel, everything is almost done and then I'll be gone and all aspersions will fly away like little birds," God said, fluttering her hands. "And by the way, you two falling in love, that was a happy accident."

Helen and Bel both let out a sigh of relief.

God, Megan and Rafferty went out on the back patio and had a glass of wine while Helen and Bel finished dinner. They had pork tenderloin with mushroom gravy and an avocado, artichoke and tomato salad with French bread followed by strawberry tart.

Helen noticed that Megan didn't seem overly concerned about Delphi's presence; rather they chatted about the law. God gave a long history of how the law came into being that Megan clearly found very interesting. Rafferty was horribly bored, she could tell. Helen and Bel watched like mother hens, but nothing out of the ordinary occurred except that they were having dinner with God.

After dinner in the den they had port and Cuban cigars that God had brought. Helen respectfully declined but Megan and Rafferty appeared to do quite well. Bel looked perfect smoking a cigar. God thanked Bel for her hospitality and left. The girls said good-bye shortly thereafter.

Rafferty and Megan were in the car when God made her appearance. "Yikes!" Rafferty said when she looked in the rearview mirror.

Megan turned around to find God lounging in the back seat of Rafferty's car.

"I need to talk to you two but there didn't seem a right time with your mothers sitting like hens watching their chicks." God handed over a piece of paper with the name *Trustworthy* scribbled on it.

Rafferty looked at her, puzzled.

"It's a horse, a ten-to-one long shot. I want you to bet ten thousand on it and the ranch will be yours, but you have to share part of it with another friend of mine. Her name is Gigi Montaine. You'll like her, she's a lot like you. Think of her as the sister you never had."

"What! Why do I have to share it?"

"It's part of the deal," God whispered. "We'll work out the details later. Don't let me down."

"Like I would dream of it," Rafferty snapped. "I knew having you as an imaginary friend would bite me in the ass one day."

"Look, you're getting your dream. Don't bitch."

"I really get the ranch?"

Megan could tell the dream was dancing around in Rafferty's head but all she could think about was how Bel was going to take it. It wasn't going to be pretty.

"Yes, I need it."

"Why?" Rafferty asked. Megan could tell she was instantly suspicious.

"It's a special place that will serve as a center for spiritual growth."

"I'm not having some sprout-eating, dope-smoking, hippie commune out there," Rafferty replied.

"It won't be. It'll be a dude ranch."

"A dude ranch?"

"Yeah." God leaned back in the seat. "I think we'd better get out of here. We've been in the drive a little too long. Can we drive to the Preserve and look at the lights? I like the city lights. They make the city look all warm and fuzzy."

"Night time is when most crime occurs," Megan stated.

"I know but I like to pretend. Can we have the top down?"

"Anything else?" Rafferty said as she pushed the button and the top started its descent.

"So you're thinking of some kind of undercover spirituality retreat," Megan inquired.

"Precisely."

They drove to the top of the Preserve, which sat on the outskirts of Phoenix, and gazed down at the lights.

"You know, I never really believed in God until now," Megan said. "I mean, my mom took me to the synagogue a few times but that was the extent of my spiritual education. I guess they couldn't decide on how much religious education I needed so I didn't get any."

"Ditto. My mom hated the Catholic church so we didn't go. Like I cared," Rafferty said.

God put her arms around them. "There is one thing you need to remember, and that is that I am in you and you are in me. The light that shines in me, shines in you."

"How beautiful is that?" Megan said.

"I just feel sorry for the poor fuckers who believe without seeing," Rafferty said.

Megan poked her in the ribs.

God laughed. "But those are the ones that will come to the ranch to discover the light."

"All right, I guess this hippie thing will be all right."

They left the lights behind and drove into town. They dropped God off in front of the homeless shelter on Thomas.

"Are you sure you want to go in there?" Rafferty asked.

"Yes, I like to spend my Sundays here. I like to think I might change something for these people in the next week."

As they drove off Megan looked over at Rafferty and said, "Bel's going to kill you."

Rafferty shrugged. "I don't know which is worse, Delphi's condemnation or my mother's."

Megan took Rafferty's hand. "But the upside of this plan is that I get to live with you in a beautiful spot and see you in tight Wrangler jeans. I'm convinced that's as close to heaven as I'll ever need."

Rafferty breathed a sigh of contentment.

"I do have an idea to soften the blow," Megan said.

Rafferty perked up. "You do?"

"Yes, we make sure Eileen hears where we're going and she'll make sure to tell Bel." Eileen, their receptionist at the law firm, would love to know she and Rafferty were headed to the races on a workday.

"And that will set the whole thing up."

"Yes."

"You're a genius."

"No, I just handle your mother better than you do."

It was hot that Monday afternoon as Megan and Rafferty stood under the awning that shaded the seats at the racetrack. They had arrived thirty minutes before the race started because Rafferty wanted to check out the horses. She was studying them through her binoculars.

"Okay, let's go place our bet," Rafferty said.

Between the two of them they had scraped up ten thousand dollars. Both of their checking accounts were drained and whatever they had in their savings accounts. Rafferty had taken a cash advance on her credit card to make up the difference.

"Is it a good horse?" Megan asked.

"Not really. He's kind of small and rather timid. Those aren't positive attributes for a racehorse."

They went to place their bet. The man behind the counter didn't say anything as Rafferty set down a ten-thousand-dollar cashier's check, but Megan could tell he was skeptical. Still, it was their money and they could do as they pleased. They went back up to the stands and waited for the race to begin. Megan was looking through the binoculars when God showed up.

"How's it going?" God said.

Megan swung around and looked at God through the binoculars. Her nostrils were the size of nickels and her teeth looked like playing cards. "Jesus!"

"Another one of my favorites," God said, taking her hand and lowering the binoculars.

"Thanks," Megan said, recovering.

"I didn't know you were coming," Rafferty said.

"Like I would miss this." God stuck her hands in the pockets of her linen blazer. She was impeccably dressed in tan pants, a white shirt and a black bowler.

"See, I wanted an outfit like that," Megan said.

"It's hot out here and besides, we didn't exactly have time to shop," Rafferty said, taking the binoculars from God. The race was about to begin.

God waved down the guy selling peanuts. "You two want some?"

"I couldn't possibly eat at a time like this," Rafferty said.

"No, thanks," Megan said.

The starting gun fired and the horses took off. Trustworthy got off to a bad start and bad went to worse.

"Are you sure about this horse?" Rafferty said.

"Oh, yes. This is where the fun part starts. Just wait," God said, popping a peanut in her mouth. Just then Trustworthy got a burst of speed and cruised past the other horses until he was neck and neck with the leader. The announcer was having an orgasm and Megan and Rafferty stood in disbelief. God smiled. Trustworthy took two giant leaps and won the race by a nose. The crowd was in an uproar. Megan and Rafferty hugged each other and jumped up and down.

"What did I tell you, oh ye of little faith. Now go get your money."

Later that afternoon Bel stood in the middle of the reception area looking for Megan and Rafferty. She was supposed to be meeting with them at this moment. "Where are they?"

"Where are who?" Eileen asked.

"Rafferty and Megan. We had a meeting scheduled for ten minutes ago and they seem to have gone missing."

"They're at the horse races," Eileen said knowingly.

"Excuse me?"

"They went to the track about an hour and a half ago. They should be back any moment."

When Rafferty and Megan came walking in, they were laughing and very excited. It appeared Bel was not happy. "And just what were you two doing at the horse races in the middle of a workday?"

"Placing a bet," Rafferty said.

"Betting?" Bel said incredulously. "Into my office, now."

"Well, of course, that's what people do at the horse races," Rafferty said as they took a seat in Bel's office. Megan knew that Rafferty was attempting to summon a sense of false confidence. It was as if the exuberance of her dream quickly faded as she stood looking at her mother.

"How much did you bet?" Bel asked with a frown.

Megan and Rafferty exchanged looks. It was now or never.

"Ten thousand," Rafferty said in her best offhand manner.

"What! Did you lose?"

"No, we won."

"What were the odds?"

"It was a long shot, ten-to-one odds," Rafferty replied. Megan watched as Bel did the math.

"You won a hundred thousand dollars?" She was pacing in front of the window.

"Well, it's not exactly mine. I did it for Delphi. I have to do something specific with the money."

"She's behind this," Bel said, her eyes narrowing. "What are you supposed to do?"

"It's kind of complicated," Rafferty said.

"Enlighten me." Bel put her hands on her hips and Megan felt her stomach drop. She could only imagine how Rafferty was feeling.

Bel perched herself on the corner of her desk. It was a power-plus-anger pose and Megan knew this meant trouble. This was the biggest moment of their lives and Megan could tell Rafferty was scared shitless.

"So?" Bel prodded.

"I'm supposed to buy this ranch."

"What ranch?"

"The one where I board my horses."

Megan could tell by the look on Bel's face that this didn't sit well. She thought she knew everything about Rafferty and now that this had come to light she was not happy.

"You have horses?"

"I'm learning to barrel race."

"How long has this been going on?"

"A couple of years," Rafferty replied. Megan watched Bel's face. She knew that Rafferty was holding the scissors to cut the apron strings and yet she was wondering which one of them would cut them first. Bel did not like secrets.

"So you're supposed to buy this ranch and do what?"

"We're supposed to make it a dude ranch."

"And this is the plan? What about your law career?"

"I would be leaving," Rafferty said. Megan could feel the axe come down. Bel would be furious and there was a good chance she would cut them out of her life permanently. Bel was like that.

"To become a cowgirl," Bel said with an acid tone in her voice.

"Something like that."

"I see." Bel got up.

"Where are you going?" Rafferty said in a panic.

"To have a word with God."

"Mom . . ."

"You'll have to excuse me but I've had enough explanations for one day."

"What are we going to do?" Megan asked after Bel left.

"Wait it out. She was pretty mad when she found out I was gay and we got past that." Rafferty put her feet up on the coffee table in Bel's office. She took a deep breath.

"But this doesn't compare."

"I know. I'm worried," Rafferty said, taking her Palm Pilot out of her pocket.

"What are you doing?"

"Programming it to see how long it'll take before she speaks to me again. This is big."

"This is really big."

Bel was still crying when God walked in. When Bel had called from the parking garage of her office building, Helen had told her God was coming in for an appointment. Helen was trying to comfort her but to no avail. "Why did she go to law school if all she wants to do is ride a horse?"

Helen refrained from saying, "To please you." She had decided it was best in their relationship not to give advice on how to handle Rafferty. She and Bel would finally sort out what needed to be done with their odd togetherness. Helen hadn't counted on that time being now or under such extreme circumstances.

"Oh, my," God said, taking a seat next to Bel on the couch and handing her the Kleenex box. "I see we're not taking the news very well."

Helen nodded as Bel started a new torrent of tears. "And then she hid this whole horse business from me like I'm some sort of jealous, controlling monster. I would have bought her a damn horse if she'd wanted one so badly. Maybe I'd like to see her ride, but no, she slinks around."

"You're not a monster, Bel," Helen said. "Sometimes, we keep quiet about things that are close to our hearts because then they remain special, if only for a short while. Remember how we didn't tell the girls about us?"

"Yes," Bel said, staring at Helen. "I wanted it to be my special little moment."

"Exactly."

"And I knew Rafferty was going to be furious when she found out," Bel said, starting to cry again.

"Let me try," God said, exasperated. "Bel, this is her dream. She hid it from you because she loves you and didn't want to disappoint you."

"But a dude ranch? That won't fly. I accepted her being gay and feared for her life from some horrid hate crime—now this."

"It's going to work," God assured her.

"How?" Bel slumped down on the couch. She looked perfectly miserable.

"Sperm."

"Sperm?"

"Racehorse sperm, to be exact."

"Rafferty doesn't know anything about stud fees and horse-breeding."

"But she does," God said.

Bel started to sob again. "I don't even know my own daughter anymore."

"What I mean is she'll learn and then she'll have all the things she needs and more."

Bel looked skeptical.

"Oy. I'm God. I can do things. All right, I admit there've been screw-ups, but I've got this one down. Bel, she's the light of your life, not an indentured servant—even she'll become free at some point. It's time," God said, handing her another tissue.

Megan sat on the corner of Rafferty's desk, which for some odd reason was amazingly tidy. Usually her desk looked like someone had put a bomb in the center of it and blown papers everywhere, and like most untidy people, Rafferty claimed to know where everything was located.

"How long has it been?" Megan asked.

Rafferty looked at her Palm Pilot. She had set the timer the moment Bel left the office in a huff. She told Megan that she'd set her alarm clock when she was younger in order to chart the length of time she could stay away from her mother. This had been the longest. "Seventy-two hours, twelve minutes and thirty-five seconds, to be exact. This is officially the longest fight we've ever had. This doesn't give me good vibes."

Megan sighed heavily. "How much longer can she hold out? Are you scared?"

"Petrified. It's hard when your dream comes true and you're not really ready. This is big. I mean, we hardly know these people we're sharing property with. Caroline will be a great help with her background in business management, but Gigi, she's out there. Do you really think this is going to work?" Rafferty rubbed her eyes. Megan knew they both needed some sleep but they'd been nervous, so insomnia had become their new best friend. They must have watched five movies in the last few nights. Thank goodness it was Friday.

"The woman upstairs seems to think so."

"Do you ever think about how freaky this is?"

"Yes, but I think it's sweet that she hasn't given up on us."

Bel suddenly appeared in the doorway. "Rafferty and Megan, a word."

Megan got up. She quietly closed the door. Her heart was racing. Bel took a seat in Rafferty's office then changed her mind and went over to the window and stared out for a moment. Megan suspected she was gathering her thoughts, most likely for an onslaught none of them was truly ready for.

The silence was excruciating. Finally Rafferty blurted, "Mom, I'm sorry I hurt you. I should've told you about the horses. I just didn't think you'd like the idea."

Bel turned slowly around. "No, I've thought about this long and hard. I should be the one who's sorry."

Megan almost fell out of her chair. Bel did not talk like this. Rafferty just sat staring in disbelief.

"I—" Rafferty started to say.

"No, listen. I've been selfish. I've held you back from things—I almost stopped you from dating Megan, and that would have been a travesty for both of us. I wanted to keep you close, to protect you from the evil world, and that wasn't fair to you. So I accept your decision."

"Really?"

"Really." Bel smiled.

"You get to keep Megan and we'll still see each other a lot. Besides, Megan is a much better lawyer than I am."

"You would be if you applied yourself. I'm sure you'll make a great cowgirl."

"You almost said that without wincing," Rafferty said, getting up.

"I'll get used to it."

Rafferty took all the tidy piles of legal documents and threw them up in the air. They come down in a shower of white.

Bel laughed. "I guess we're done with that."

"I love you," Rafferty said, giving her a huge hug.

"I don't think I've ever seen you this happy." Bel wrapped her arms around her. Megan smiled. This was truly a momentous occasion.

"I've never been this happy and it's because of you. Thanks, Mom."

"Now go buy your ranch and I expect the first dinner invitation," Bel said, bending over to pick up the papers.

Megan and Rafferty fairly skipped out of the office.

Chapter Thirteen

When Megan and Rafferty got to the title company office Gigi was sitting in the lobby with her head between her knees. Caroline had her hand on Gigi's back. Their shoes made almost no noise on the heavy plush carpet that lined the lobby. Everything was decorated in muted burgundy tones.

"What's wrong with her?" Rafferty asked.

"She's having a panic attack." Caroline shrugged.

"This is just fucking great. Where the hell is Delphi when you need her?" Rafferty said, pulling her frazzled hair into a ponytail.

"She might be kind of busy. She probably assumes that we can handle it," Megan said. A month had passed since they won the money and made their deal with God.

"I don't think we're doing a very good job of it at the moment," Caroline said, eyeing Gigi as she got up and spit in the nearest trash can. She had a dry heave and a couple passing by stopped and stared.

Gigi came back and sat with her head in her hands. "Oh, I feel terrible."

Rafferty squatted down next to her and lifted up her head in a no-nonsense manner. Megan agreed it was time to take action. Rafferty was not going to be this close to her dream and have a pipsqueak with a bad stomach ruin everything. "Gigi, sweetie darling, I just quit my job at the law firm, horrified my mother and put my whole life on the line here, so if anyone should be having a panic attack here it would be me. I don't think quitting your job as a photographer of auras for New Age nutballs is in the same category. So buck up and let's get on with this."

Horrified, Megan looked at Rafferty. This was not a good start to the partnership. They had just spent the last month buying the ranch and getting everything legally organized, which had been no small task.

"What?" Rafferty said. "It's true, isn't it? She needs to get up and get with the program. Take a few deep breaths and let's roll."

"Rafferty!" Megan said. "That was a little harsh."

"No, she's right," Gigi said, straightening her shoulders and then standing up. "I can do this."

"Great, let's go," Rafferty said. She put her arm through Gigi's. "You know, you and I have a lot in common—we're both shits—so this might just work out."

Gigi smiled. "I think you have bigger balls than I do."

"That's why my pants are bigger than yours."

"For all your extra equipment?" Gigi asked.

They all laughed.

"Yep, pretty soon I'll need a dolly just to carry it all around," Rafferty said, pushing the elevator button. Megan smiled. This was the beginning of their new lives and when it was over they could go celebrate and then drive to the ranch to check it all out. She couldn't wait.

Epilogue
Two months later

They had been at the ranch two months now and Megan, Rafferty and Caroline had been working out the requisitions for all the stuff running a ranch required. They had converted one of the old ranch houses into the operations center. Caroline was off for the summer from her job as a teaching assistant in the M.B.A. program at the small-business college.

"I don't know what I would do without you. Like, I can run an Excel program. I wasn't even good at logging my hours as a lawyer. My mom used to get so mad. I like to do things, not chart them," Rafferty said.

"And boy did she get pissed," Megan piped in. She was going through a Western wear catalogue looking for some new boots.

"I know, but once I get this set up you will be so organized that you can do inventory, place your orders, pay for them and then sit back and have a cocktail in the evening and not have to worry about a thing," Caroline said, her fingers flitting across the keyboard like they were possessed.

Gigi came into the office and they all looked up.

"How do I look?" Gigi asked. She was dressed in a checkered cowboy shirt with a red bandana tied around her neck, tight Wrangler jeans and short red cowboy boots with white scrolls on them.

Caroline sat with her mouth wide open and Rafferty started to giggle.

"What?" Gigi asked.

"The truth?" Rafferty said. Megan could see she was obviously trying to compose herself.

"Yeah."

"You look absolutely absurd," Rafferty said.

"What's with the getup?" Caroline asked.

"I'm doing this talk at the Women's Center on getting your life together and about writing books. Danielle hooked me up with this gig. She says that since the community center helped me get back on track, I should share my lessons of success with other women. I thought this outfit would go great with the dude-ranch writer thing. You know, like Tony Hillerman. I want to play the part," Gigi said. She adjusted her giant silver belt buckle.

"Oh," Caroline said.

"Where'd you get that?" Rafferty asked.

"At the feed store," Gigi replied.

This started a fresh set of giggles.

"Would you like a bale of hay to go with that God-awful shirt?" Caroline said.

"Or how about some oats to go with that belt buckle the size of a dinner plate," Rafferty added.

"Or how about . . ." Caroline started.

"Hey, that's enough. I get it," Gigi said, pouting.

"Come on, you guys. Gigi is doing a good thing here, and I

think we should encourage her. But we do need to get her a new outfit," Megan said diplomatically. She then burst into a fit of laughter.

"See, you're just as bad," Rafferty said. She wiped her eyes with the sleeve of her T-shirt.

"Gigi, I've got a whole closet full of really nice business suits. We're about the same size. Let's go find you something appropriate to wear. Okay?" Megan said.

"Thanks. I do think the belt buckle is a little over the top."

"Just a bit."

Megan dug around in her closet while Gigi disrobed.

"Megan? I'm really scared. I don't think I'm up to this even if God does. This talk is supposed to be a practice session for the book tour, a promotion thing."

Megan emerged from the depths of the closet with a set of matching shoes for the tailored black suit and gray shirt. Gigi suddenly looked small and vulnerable. "Gigi, it'll be fine. The first time I went to court I was scared shitless, but you get used to it and then it becomes fun. Here, try this on."

After she finished dressing they inspected her in the long bathroom mirror.

"See, that's better. You look like a professional." Megan straightened out Gigi's collar.

"Megan, do you think Rafferty will teach me how to ride a horse?"

"Of course, but you have to promise me something." Megan handed Gigi the shoes.

"What?" Gigi asked, sitting on the corner of the bed. The shoes fit.

"No more shopping for Western wear unsupervised. I'll go with you next time."

"It's a deal."

God and Gigi were standing on the hill that overlooked the ranch. They had just finished painting all the outbuildings a light brown adobe color so they matched the big rambling house that Gigi shared with Rafferty, Megan and Caroline. The roofs had been redone in a sage green metal, and all the fencing that lined the long driveway had been painted white. It all looked like something out of Dallas.

"My goodness, this place looks stunning," God said.

"You really like it. It's taken us nearly two months and a dozen contractors later," Gigi replied. She picked a piece of grass and stuck it in her mouth.

God smiled at her. "That hat suits you," she said, indicating Gigi's straw cowboy hat.

"Megan bought it for me because she says I have poor taste in clothes."

"And she's right. She showed me that Howdy Doody outfit you almost wore to your first talk. I was mortified."

"And then you laughed hysterically."

"I almost had a seizure."

"Very funny."

"No, really, I stopped by to tell you that I'm proud of you, all of you, for making this dream of mine come to fruition."

"Does this mean you're leaving us?" Gigi asked. She had known this day would come and there had been times when she had wanted it but now, now she was used to having God around. She wasn't sure she wanted her to leave.

"Not exactly. I still have some things I want to do and I kind of like it here. You might want to keep one of those guest rooms handy in case I need a vacation. Besides, the book comes out in a week and I want a signed copy."

"Sure. But don't you think you should be the one signing it?"

"What? And get crucified?"

They both laughed.

"All right, my little cowgirl, I've got to go. You be good."

"I'll try."

"Oh, by the way, I left you some notes for your next book on your desk." God stuck her hands in her pockets and rocked back on her heels.

Gigi pulled her hat down lower on her head and groaned.

"It'll be fine."

"It makes me nervous when you say that," Gigi said.

"And that's how I like to keep you. So *hasta luego*, and behave yourself."

"I will. I mean I'll try."

"I know you will." God touched her hand and smiled.

God disappeared and left Gigi alone on the hilltop. The sun was beginning to set and everything glowed in that soft pink light that always made her wonder if God had a watercolor paintbrush that she used at the end of the day to make everything seem better. She smiled. When this whole thing started she couldn't believe it and now that it was over she still couldn't believe it. Maybe the best things in life are the hardest to make yourself believe in, Gigi thought, like dreams. But sometimes they did come true, perhaps in the presence of a God that never gave up. She walked down the hill toward the house to be with her friends and to enjoy her new life.

About the Author

Saxon Bennett lives in the East Mountains of New Mexico with her partner of sixteen years and their four furry children, two cats and two dogs. She is an avid snowboarder and resigns herself to gardening in the summer, which affords sensory pleasures but lacks the dopamine rush. We all have to make sacrifices.

Publications from
BELLA BOOKS, INC.
The best in contemporary lesbian fiction

P.O. Box 10543, Tallahassee, FL 32302
Phone: 800-729-4992
www.bellabooks.com

TALK OF THE TOWN TOO by Saxon Bennett. 181 pp. Second in the series about wild and fun loving friends. ISBN 1-931513-77-5 $12.95

LOVE SPEAKS HER NAME by Laura DeHart Young. 170 pp. Love and friendship, desire and intrigue, spark this exciting sequel to *Forever and the Night*.
ISBN 1-59493-002-3 $12.95

TO HAVE AND TO HOLD by Peggy J. Herring. 184 pp. By finally letting down her defenses, will Dorian be opening herself to a devastating betrayal?
ISBN 1-59493-005-8 $12.95

WILD THINGS by Karin Kallmaker. 228 pp. Dutiful daughter Faith has met the perfect man. There's just one problem: she's in love with his sister. ISBN 1-931513-64-3 $12.95

SHARED WINDS by Kenna White. 216 pp. Can Emma rebuild more than just Lanny's marina? ISBN 1-59493-006-6 $12.95

THE UNKNOWN MILE by Jaime Clevenger. 253 pp. Kelly's world is getting more and more complicated every moment. ISBN 1-931513-57-0 $12.95

TREASURED PAST by Linda Hill. 189 pp. A shared passion for antiques leads to love.
ISBN 1-59493-003-1 $12.95

SIERRA CITY by Gerri Hill. 284 pp. Chris and Jesse cannot deny their growing attraction . . . ISBN 1-931513-98-8 $12.95

ALL THE WRONG PLACES by Karin Kallmaker. 174 pp. Sex and the single girl—Brandy is looking for love and usually she finds it. Karin Kallmaker's first *After Dark* erotic novel. ISBN 1-931513-76-7 $12.95

WHEN THE CORPSE LIES A Motor City Thriller by Therese Szymanski. 328 pp. Butch bad-girl Brett Higgins is used to waking up next to beautiful women she hardly knows. Problem is, this one's dead. ISBN 1-931513-74-0 $12.95

GUARDED HEARTS by Hannah Rickard. 240 pp. Someone's reminding Alyssa about her secret past, and then she becomes the suspect in a series of burglaries.
ISBN 1-931513-99-6 $12.95

ONCE MORE WITH FEELING by Peggy J. Herring. 184 pp. Lighthearted, loving, romantic adventure. ISBN 1-931513-60-0 $12.95

TANGLED AND DARK A Brenda Strange Mystery by Patty G. Henderson. 240 pp. When investigating a local death, Brenda finds two possible killers—one diagnosed with Multiple Personality Disorder. ISBN 1-931513-75-9 $12.95

WHITE LACE AND PROMISES by Peggy J. Herring. 240 pp. Maxine and Betina realize sex may not be the most important thing in their lives. ISBN 1-931513-73-2 $12.95

UNFORGETTABLE by Karin Kallmaker. 288 pp. Can Rett find love with the cheerleader who broke her heart so many years ago? ISBN 1-931513-63-5 $12.95

HIGHER GROUND by Saxon Bennett. 280 pp. A delightfully complex reflection of the successful, high society lives of a small group of women. ISBN 1-931513-69-4 $12.95

LAST CALL A Detective Franco Mystery by Baxter Clare. 240 pp. Frank overlooks all else to try to solve a cold case of two murdered children... ISBN 1-931513-70-8 $12.95

ONCE UPON A DYKE: NEW EXPLOITS OF FAIRY-TALE LESBIANS by Karin Kallmaker, Julia Watts, Barbara Johnson & Therese Szymanski. 320 pp. You've never read fairy tales like these before! From Bella After Dark. ISBN 1-931513-71-6 $14.95

FINEST KIND OF LOVE by Diana Tremain Braund. 224 pp. Can Molly and Carolyn stop clashing long enough to see beyond their differences? ISBN 1-931513-68-6 $12.95

DREAM LOVER by Lyn Denison. 188 pp. A soft, sensuous, romantic fantasy.
ISBN 1-931513-96-1 $12.95

NEVER SAY NEVER by Linda Hill. 224 pp. A classic love story… where rules aren't the only things broken. ISBN 1-931513-67-8 $12.95

PAINTED MOON by Karin Kallmaker. 214 pp. Stranded together in a snowbound cabin, Jackie and Leah's lives will never be the same. ISBN 1-931513-53-8 $12.95

WIZARD OF ISIS by Jean Stewart. 240 pp. Fifth in the exciting Isis series.
ISBN 1-931513-71-4 $12.95

WOMAN IN THE MIRROR by Jackie Calhoun. 216 pp. Josey learns to love again, while her niece is learning to love women for the first time. ISBN 1-931513-78-3 $12.95

SUBSTITUTE FOR LOVE by Karin Kallmaker. 200 pp. When Holly and Reyna meet the combination adds up to pure passion. But what about tomorrow? ISBN 1-931513-62-7 $12.95

GULF BREEZE by Gerri Hill. 288 pp. Could Carly really be the woman Pat has always been searching for? ISBN 1-931513-97-X $12.95

THE TOMSTOWN INCIDENT by Penny Hayes. 184 pp. Caught between two worlds, Eloise must make a decision that will change her life forever. ISBN 1-931513-56-2 $12.95

MAKING UP FOR LOST TIME by Karin Kallmaker. 240 pp. Discover delicious recipes for romance by the undisputed mistress. ISBN 1-931513-61-9 $12.95

THE WAY LIFE SHOULD BE by Diana Tremain Braund. 173 pp. With which woman will Jennifer find the true meaning of love? ISBN 1-931513-66-X $12.95

BACK TO BASICS: A BUTCH/FEMME ANTHOLOGY edited by Therese Szymanski—from Bella After Dark. 324 pp. ISBN 1-931513-35-X $14.95

SURVIVAL OF LOVE by Frankie J. Jones. 236 pp. What will Jody do when she falls in love with her best friend's daughter? ISBN 1-931513-55-4 $12.95

LESSONS IN MURDER by Claire McNab. 184 pp. 1st Detective Inspector Carol Ashton Mystery.   ISBN 1-931513-65-1 $12.95

DEATH BY DEATH by Claire McNab. 167 pp. 5th Denise Cleever Thriller.   ISBN 1-931513-34-1 $12.95

CAUGHT IN THE NET by Jessica Thomas. 188 pp. A wickedly observant story of mystery, danger, and love in Provincetown.   ISBN 1-931513-54-6 $12.95

DREAMS FOUND by Lyn Denison. Australian Riley embarks on a journey to meet her birth mother . . . and gains not just a family, but the love of her life.   ISBN 1-931513-58-9 $12.95

A MOMENT'S INDISCRETION by Peggy J. Herring. 154 pp. Jackie is torn between her better judgment and the overwhelming attraction she feels for Valerie.   ISBN 1-931513-59-7 $12.95

IN EVERY PORT by Karin Kallmaker. 224 pp. Jessica has a woman in every port. Will meeting Cat change all that?   ISBN 1-931513-36-8 $12.95

TOUCHWOOD by Karin Kallmaker. 240 pp. Rayann loves Louisa. Louisa loves Rayann. Can the decades between their ages keep them apart?   ISBN 1-931513-37-6 $12.95

WATERMARK by Karin Kallmaker. 248 pp. Teresa wants a future with a woman whose heart has been frozen by loss. Sequel to *Touchwood*.   ISBN 1-931513-38-4 $12.95

EMBRACE IN MOTION by Karin Kallmaker. 240 pp. Has Sarah found lust or love?   ISBN 1-931513-39-2 $12.95

ONE DEGREE OF SEPARATION by Karin Kallmaker. 232 pp. Sizzling small town romance between Marian, the town librarian, and the new girl from the big city.   ISBN 1-931513-30-9 $12.95

CRY HAVOC A Detective Franco Mystery by Baxter Clare. 240 pp. A dead hustler with a headless rooster in his lap sends Lt. L.A. Franco headfirst against Mother Love.   ISBN 1-931513931-7 $12.95

DISTANT THUNDER by Peggy J. Herring. 294 pp. Bankrobbing drifter Cordy awakens strange new feelings in Leo in this romantic tale set in the Old West.   ISBN 1-931513-28-7 $12.95

COP OUT by Claire McNab. 216 pp. 4th Detective Inspector Carol Ashton Mystery.   ISBN 1-931513-29-5 $12.95

BLOOD LINK by Claire McNab. 159 pp. 15th Detective Inspector Carol Ashton Mystery. Is Carol unwittingly playing into a deadly plan?   ISBN 1-931513-27-9 $12.95

TALK OF THE TOWN by Saxon Bennett. 239 pp. With enough beer, barbecue and B.S., anything is possible!   ISBN 1-931513-18-X $12.95

MAYBE NEXT TIME by Karin Kallmaker. 256 pp. Sabrina has everything she ever wanted—except Jorie.   ISBN 1-931513-26-0 $12.95

WHEN GOOD GIRLS GO BAD: A Motor City Thriller by Therese Szymanski. 230 pp. Brett, Randi, and Allie join forces to stop a serial killer.   ISBN 1-931513-11-2 $12.95

A DAY TOO LONG: A Helen Black Mystery by Pat Welch. 328 pp. This time Helen's fate is in her own hands.   ISBN 1-931513-22-8 $12.95

THE RED LINE OF YARMALD by Diana Rivers. 256 pp. The Hadra's only hope lies in a magical red line . . . climactic sequel to *Clouds of War*. ISBN 1-931513-23-6 $12.95

OUTSIDE THE FLOCK by Jackie Calhoun. 224 pp. Jo embraces her new love and life. ISBN 1-931513-13-9 $12.95

LEGACY OF LOVE by Marianne K. Martin. 224 pp. Read the whole Sage Bristo story. ISBN 1-931513-15-5 $12.95

STREET RULES: A Detective Franco Mystery by Baxter Clare. 304 pp. Gritty, fast-paced mystery with compelling Detective L.A. Franco ISBN 1-931513-14-7 $12.95

RECOGNITION FACTOR: 4th Denise Cleever Thriller by Claire McNab. 176 pp. Denise Cleever tracks a notorious terrorist to America. ISBN 1-931513-24-4 $12.95

NORA AND LIZ by Nancy Garden. 296 pp. Lesbian romance by the author of *Annie on My Mind*. ISBN 1931513-20-1 $12.95

MIDAS TOUCH by Frankie J. Jones. 208 pp. Sandra had everything but love. ISBN 1-931513-21-X $12.95

BEYOND ALL REASON by Peggy J. Herring. 240 pp. A romance hotter than Texas. ISBN 1-9513-25-2 $12.95

ACCIDENTAL MURDER: 14th Detective Inspector Carol Ashton Mystery by Claire McNab. 208 pp. Carol Ashton tracks an elusive killer. ISBN 1-931513-16-3 $12.95

SEEDS OF FIRE: Tunnel of Light Trilogy, Book 2 by Karin Kallmaker writing as Laura Adams. 274 pp. In Autumn's dreams no one is who they seem. ISBN 1-931513-19-8 $12.95

DRIFTING AT THE BOTTOM OF THE WORLD by Auden Bailey. 288 pp. Beautifully written first novel set in Antarctica. ISBN 1-931513-17-1 $12.95

CLOUDS OF WAR by Diana Rivers. 288 pp. Women unite to defend Zelindar! ISBN 1-931513-12-0 $12.95

DEATHS OF JOCASTA: 2nd Micky Knight Mystery by J.M. Redmann. 408 pp. Sexy and intriguing Lambda Literary Award–nominated mystery. ISBN 1-931513-10-4 $12.95

LOVE IN THE BALANCE by Marianne K. Martin. 256 pp. The classic lesbian love story, back in print! ISBN 1-931513-08-2 $12.95

THE COMFORT OF STRANGERS by Peggy J. Herring. 272 pp. Lela's work was her passion . . . until now. ISBN 1-931513-09-0 $12.95

CHICKEN by Paula Martinac. 208 pp. Lynn finds that the only thing harder than being in a lesbian relationship is ending one. ISBN 1-931513-07-4 $11.95

TAMARACK CREEK by Jackie Calhoun. 208 pp. An intriguing story of love and danger. ISBN 1-931513-06-6 $11.95

DEATH BY THE RIVERSIDE: 1st Micky Knight Mystery by J.M. Redmann. 320 pp. Finally back in print, the book that launched the Lambda Literary Award–winning Micky Knight mystery series. ISBN 1-931513-05-8 $11.95

EIGHTH DAY: A Cassidy James Mystery by Kate Calloway. 272 pp. In the eighth installment of the Cassidy James mystery series, Cassidy goes undercover at a camp for troubled teens. ISBN 1-931513-04-X $11.95